PENNY WISE

Penny can't wait to go on the holiday of a lifetime with her best friend, Angela. But then comes some terrible news: her father has had a heart-attack. Now she will have to spend the summer looking after her parents' little seaside shop instead. That wouldn't be so bad but the neighbouring LoPrice supermarket has its eyes on the property. And Penny isn't sure what to make of the assistant manager, Graham Fraser. He's young, good-looking — and very ambitious.

EWAN SMITH

◆

PENNY WISE

Complete and Unabridged

LINFORD
Leicester

First published in Great Britain in 2018

First Linford Edition
published 2021

A catalogue record for this book is available
from the British Library.

ISBN 978–1–4448–4729–1

Published by
Ulverscroft Limited
Anstey, Leicestershire

Printed and bound in Great Britain by
TJ Books Ltd., Padstow, Cornwall

This book is printed on acid-free paper

EWAN SMITH

◆

PENNY WISE

Complete and Unabridged

LINFORD
Leicester

First published in Great Britain in 2018

First Linford Edition
published 2021

A catalogue record for this book is available
from the British Library.

ISBN 978–1–4448–4729–1

Published by
Ulverscroft Limited
Anstey, Leicestershire

Printed and bound in Great Britain by
TJ Books Ltd., Padstow, Cornwall

This book is printed on acid-free paper

Shattered Dreams

Penny sat up on the sun lounger, peering critically at her toenails as seagulls cried in the background. She lifted her sunglasses to get a better look.

'I thought painting each toenail with a different design would look pretty cool. But now I'm thinking it looks ...'

'Pretty weird?' Angela suggested with a grin.

She turned back to her phone and tapped a few buttons. The noise of the seagulls disappeared, to be replaced by the sound of waves lapping gently against the beach.

'That's better,' she said in satisfaction.

She turned up the volume and settled back in her deckchair.

Penny picked up her cocktail.

'This is the life.' She gazed through the window at the grey sky outside and imagined it a dazzling, cloudless blue. They were in Angela's cramped university bedsit and the two friends were getting in some practice for the summer holidays.

In less than a fortnight, they would be heading off to the Mediterranean sun and they were eagerly counting down the days.

In September, they would both be starting their final year at university, so this summer would be their last chance to really enjoy life before they became engulfed by the world of work and responsibility. They intended to make the most of it.

'*Comment ça va?*' Penny asked.

Angela smiled.

'*Très bien!*'

Penny stretched out on her sun lounger.

'It's going to be so brilliant when we get to France. The food, the culture …'

'The men,' Angela murmured.

Penny sighed happily.

'It's such a romantic country. Who knows what might happen.'

'I'll drink to that.' They clinked glasses.

'To the holiday of a lifetime.'

Their plans were vague. They simply intended to travel and have fun. They would start by making their way through France, then perhaps to Spain, and Italy, and Greece.

If their money ran short, they could always pick up a bit of bar work or do some fruit picking to keep them going. They would wander wherever the fancy took them and hope that the summer never ended.

A smile played about Penny's mouth.

'Oh, Angela, just two weeks to go.'

'Angelique,' Angela murmured.

'What?'

'Angelique. I think I'll change my name to Angelique for the summer.'

Penny's eyes widened.

'That's a brilliant idea! I'll change my name to, to …'

'Paris!'

Their laughter filled the little room as Penny's phone gave a chirrup. She looked at the screen and pressed a key.

'Hi, Mum. How's things?'

The easy smile was suddenly wiped from her face as she heard the panic in her mother's voice.

'Oh, Penny, it's your dad. He's had a heart attack!'

* * *

'I'm so glad you're here, Penny,' Maisie cried, her cheeks glistening with tears. She clutched at her daughter. 'It's been such a terrible time.'

'Shh,' Penny murmured. She rubbed her Mum's back gently, comforting her as if she was the mother instead of the other way round. 'Don't worry. It'll be fine.'

Penny was exhausted. Everything had gone wrong on her journey – trains being delayed, bus timetables out of date, taxis getting lost. It had seemed to take for ever before she finally got to Weale-On-Sea and all the time she had been worried to bits about her dad.

In the end, the news wasn't nearly as bad as it might have been.

'Your dad is all right,' Auntie May had reassured her when she picked Penny up at the bus station. 'Fortunately, the ambulance crew got to the shop really quickly. They whizzed your dad straight to the hospital, which was the best possible place for him.'

However, it was clear to Penny that her mum was struggling to cope.

'I've always told Bill that he works too hard at the shop,' Maisie said, dabbing at her eyes with a sodden tissue. 'He shouldn't be lifting and carrying at his age.'

For as long as Penny could remember, her mum and dad had run All And Sundry, a little shop near the beach at Weale-On-Sea.

It was a bit of a café, a bit of a hardware store, a bit of a grocery shop — a bit of everything, really.

Maisie shook her head.

'Bill decided that the windows needed cleaning. I told him it was ridiculous — the cleaner was due any day. But he wouldn't listen. When he got the ladder and bucket out, I knew there was something wrong.

'He was snappy with me, which he never usually is, and his face was a funny colour.

Then he got halfway up the ladder and just stopped. I asked if there was something wrong and he turned to me …' Maisie clutched her daughter's arm.

'Penny, that look in his eyes, I don't think I'll ever forget it. The bucket dropped from his fingers. I ran over and managed to grab him before he fell, but he was so heavy.

Two of the customers helped me to lie him down on the pavement and someone called the ambulance, I don't know who.'

Maisie turned a tear-stained face.

'I was so scared, Penny. I didn't know what to do.'

★ ★ ★

Penny sat with her Auntie May in the hospital café with a pot of tea between them. They had wanted Maisie to come, too, but she wouldn't leave Bill's side for a moment. Penny let out a weary yawn.

'I am so tired.'

Auntie May smiled sympathetically.

'Travelling always has that effect. And you had the worry of your dad as well.'

Penny shook her head.

'It was all I could think of on the journey.'

Auntie May placed a hand gently on her arm.

'I've spoken to the doctor. Your dad is going to be fine. The speed of the ambulance crew made a real difference.

Tests will be done to work out what the problem is exactly and then they'll decide the best treatment for the future. But it doesn't look as if there should be any long-term effects from the heart attack.'

'Do they have any idea how long he'll be in hospital?' Penny asked.

Auntie May shrugged.

'It's not definite yet. He'll certainly be kept in for a few days so that they can keep an eye on him. But if everything goes as they hope then he'll probably get out sometime early next week.'

'It's not going to be easy for Mum. Dad is the worst patient in the world.'

'That was something the doctor mentioned. When he does get home, it's essential that he takes things easy. He'll need rest and relaxation and to avoid stress at all costs.'

★ ★ ★

'This is such nonsense — there's nothing wrong with me.' Bill tried to push himself up in bed. 'I strained my shoulder carrying the ladder and bucket. That was the cause of the pain in my chest.'

'Bill, for goodness sake, lie back,' Maisie cried. 'You'll just make things worse.'

'There's nothing to make worse. It's ridiculous that I'm being kept here in hospital. I thought they were short of beds. Surely there's someone needing this one more than me?'

A nurse strode over with an icy glare

on her face.

'What's this noise all about? We're in a hospital ward — not some rowdy bar.'

'I'm just saying ...' Bill began.

'Try listening instead,' the nurse retorted. 'As Mrs Sullivan has just made clear, you need to lie back on that bed and stop causing a fuss.'

'But there's nothing wrong with me.'

The nurse fixed him with narrowed eyes.

'How long have you studied medicine, Mr Sullivan?'

Bill frowned.

'What do you mean?'

'Doctor Sangar has had six years of medical training and twenty years of clinical practice. He wants you lying in bed for the next couple of days while tests are done and your treatment is agreed. But you know better than him, do you?'

'Of course I don't, but ...'

'But nothing. Lie there quietly until you are told otherwise. Is — that — clear?'

9

Bill's eyes dropped under the nurse's glare.

'Yes, that's clear,' he muttered.

'Good. Now I don't want to hear any more fuss from this part of the ward for the rest of the evening. I have work to do.'

She turned on her heel and strode off.

They watched her go in silence and Auntie May let out a quiet whistle.

'I didn't think they still made nurses like that.'

Maisie began tucking the sheets round her husband.

'I hope you were paying attention.'

Bill gave an irritable sigh.

'How can I lie here in bed, day after day? I have a shop to run.'

Maisie gazed at him in horror.

'What are you thinking, Bill? You can't run the shop at the moment. You're not well.'

'If I don't, then who will? You can't manage it by yourself.'

'There's Flo,' Penny suggested.

10

Bill waved his hand dismissively.

'Flo is a great worker and we would never have managed without her all these years. But she could no more look after All And Sundry than she could fly to the moon. She's just not up to it.'

Penny knew that was true. Flo baked lemon drizzle cake to die for but she would never be able to cope with the responsibility of running the shop.

Maisie shrugged.

'All And Sundry will just have to close until you get better.'

'That's impossible,' Bill spluttered.

'Business is bad enough as it is. If we close the shop at this time of year, we might as well give it up completely.'

Penny felt like suggesting that they did just that. It was time that her mum and dad retired. The business had been failing for years. They worked so hard at it but it barely made them a living.

On the other hand, she knew how her dad would react to such an idea.

'I don't care what you say, Bill. You're not going back to work until you're completely better.'

Penny smiled at the determination in Maisie's voice. Her mum seemed to have adopted some of the nurse's firmness.

'So, what are we going to do?'

There was a sound from Penny's phone. She looked down. It was a text from Angela.

She gave a quiet sigh. It didn't seem possible that only yesterday the two of them had been getting ready for their summer adventure.

Hope your dad is OK, the message read. *Don't worry about our holiday. If you can't manage it, I completely understand. Angela (Angelique!) xxx*

Penny felt her eyes blurring. She and Angela had been planning the holiday for so long. It was going to be such fun.

'So what will we do about the shop?' Bill demanded again.

As Penny put her phone away, she felt something in her pocket. It was the sunglasses she'd been wearing just the day before. She gazed at them gloomily. She knew what she would have to do.

She forced a smile on to her face and turned brightly to her mum and dad.

'Don't worry about the shop. I can take care of it over the summer. I'll look after it until you're both ready to get back to work.'

A Prickly Encounter

Penny strode along the promenade, the shop keys jingling in her pocket. The previous evening, the argument over what should happen with All And Sundry had dragged on and on.

Bill had been determined. He would have a day or two in his hospital bed if absolutely necessary but then he would get back to work.

'The shop has been shut for too long as it is. It will be a disaster for the business if it stays closed. Anyway, I need to be up and about. I've had enough of lazing around in bed.'

Maisie had clearly been upset by his attitude.

'You can't possibly return to work straightaway, Bill. Before you know it, you'll be back in hospital again. Or worse.'

However, Bill could be stubborn when he chose. No matter what Maisie or Auntie May or Penny said, he stuck to his guns.

Things only changed when Dr Sangar turned up. He made it clear that it was out of the question for Bill to go straight back to work.

'Two days ago, your body gave you a message, Mr Sullivan. You need to start taking things more easily.'

Bill waved a hand in disgust.

'I've still got the best years of my life ahead of me.'

Dr Sangar smiled.

'Actually, I agree with you. But you will only enjoy those years if you look after yourself.' He sat down on the bed beside Bill and looked him in the eye. 'For one thing, I want you to start thinking about your diet.'

Bill groaned.

'Don't tell me — half a grapefruit for breakfast and lettuce leaves for lunch.'

Dr Sangar gave a gentle laugh.

'I think we can be a bit more imaginative than that. We have a dietician here at the hospital and I'd like to make an appointment for you and Mrs Sullivan to have a chat with her.'

Bill began to protest but Maisie nodded firmly.

'Certainly, Doctor. We'd like to hear what she has to say.'

'And then there's exercise,' Dr Sangar continued.

'I get plenty of exercise,' Bill protested.

Maisie snorted.

'Walking to and from the Frog And Whistle.'

The doctor handed Maisie a leaflet.

'This has some useful advice to help you and Mr Sullivan introduce some simple exercises into your daily life.'

'Oh, for goodness sake,' Bill muttered.

Maisie took the leaflet.

'That sounds like an excellent idea. I'll see that we both follow it to the letter.'

Dr Sangar gazed at Bill for a moment.

'The most important thing is to give your body a chance to recover. It's had a severe shock. The last thing it needs is for you to go back to the routine which caused the problem in the first place.

You need a few weeks of gentle exercise and, most importantly, no stress.'

Bill snorted.

'No stress indeed! I'm feeling fine. And I can't possibly be away from the shop at this time of year.'

Penny put a hand on his arm.

'I told you, Dad. I'll look after the shop. I've worked in it often enough in the past.'

'That was when you were a teenager, just waiting on tables and serving on the till. Being in charge of the shop is a completely different kettle of fish.'

Penny smiled.

'I'm a big girl now. Or hadn't you noticed?'

'Anyway, what about your holiday? You and Angela have been planning it for months.'

'Angelique,' Penny murmured to herself and the feeling of gloom again settled over her. It would have been such an adventure.

She shook her head.

'Never mind about our holiday, Dad.

There'll be other summers for me and Angela. This is more important.'

Auntie May leaned forward.

'I have a suggestion, Doctor. I live in a village in the Lake District. It's such a peaceful place. Perhaps Bill and Maisie could come and stay with me for a few weeks.'

'That would be wonderful!' Maisie exclaimed.

Dr Sangar nodded.

'It sounds perfect.'

'Hang on a minute!' Bill protested.

'That's settled,' Auntie May said firmly. 'When you get out of hospital, you and Maisie will come and stay with me for an extended visit. And Penny will take care of All And Sundry.'

★   ★   ★

Penny smiled to herself. Her dad had been up against four determined people and, in the end, he had given in to the inevitable. So here she was, on her way to open the shop for the first time.

18

It wasn't even eight o'clock in the morning but already things were starting to get busy in the little resort. There were a few families wandering about the beach, even some children paddling in the shallows.

And she could see members of the Swimming For Seniors Club gathering by the pier. They were an eager lot and, in the summer, they always went for a swim first thing, no matter what the weather.

A young man at the Surfing Shack was bringing out some plastic canoes and lining them up on the sand.

'Looks like it's going to be a good day,' Penny called as she passed.

'Fingers crossed,' he replied, gazing at her with obvious admiration.

Penny carried on along the prom with a smile. She hadn't recognised him but that was hardly surprising. A lot of the tourist businesses had a high turnover of staff, often young people who worked there for the summer and then moved on.

And she hadn't spent all that much time at Weale-On-Sea over the past couple of years, just fleeting holiday visits.

She stepped to one side to allow a family group to hurry past. They were on their way to the beach and the children could barely contain their excitement.

Even at that time in the morning, there were plenty of people about, having breakfast in the cafés, playing games in the arcade, peering in the shop windows. There were lots of potential customers around for the local businesses.

She turned up Beach Road and then stopped with a grimace. Up ahead of her was All And Sundry. In comparison to the gleaming LoPrice Supermarket next door, it seemed a bit tatty and forlorn. She wondered when it had last enjoyed a lick of paint.

A puzzled look crossed her face. By the side of the shop was a sizeable area of waste ground. It belonged to All And Sundry and Bill had always planned to develop it somehow for the benefit of the business, though nothing had ever come of that.

Standing there was a smartly dressed young man with a clipboard in his hand. He seemed to be making notes and, as Penny watched, he took a phone out of his pocket and began taking pictures of the shop.

She crossed the road.

'Hi, can I help?'

He looked at her with a frown.

'And you are?'

Penny felt herself bristling. He was behaving as if he owned the place.

'My name is Penny Sullivan. This shop and this piece of ground belong to my parents.'

At once, his frown was replaced by an expression of sympathy and concern.

'I was so sorry to hear about what happened to your father. How is Bill?'

His sudden change of attitude wrong-footed Penny.

'He's fine, thanks. He's still in hospital but he's due out in a couple of days and then he and Mum are going to spend some time in the Lake District with my aunt.'

He nodded.

'That sounds like a good plan. Your mum and dad are two of the mainstays of the community here at Weale-On-Sea. It's important that they look after themselves now that they're getting on a bit.'

Penny frowned.

'They're only in their sixties.'

He smiled.

'And they deserve a long and happy retirement.'

Penny felt herself starting to get irritated again. As she knew only too well, her dad had no intention of retiring any time in the near future.

She gazed pointedly at the clipboard he was holding. Noticing her look, he stretched out a hand with a smile.

'Goodness, I haven't introduced myself yet. I'm Graham Fraser. It's good to meet you, Penny.' His hand was warm and firm. 'I'm assistant manager at LoPrice next door. We're your mum and dad's neighbours so if there's anything we can do to help then just ask.'

The offer seemed sincere and Penny returned his smile.

'That's kind of you,' she said, deciding that perhaps he wasn't so bad after all.

Graham held up his clipboard.

'I hope you don't think that I'm jumping the gun but when my boss heard that your mum and dad were going to be selling up, he suggested that I make a few preliminary notes.'

Penny looked at him in bafflement.

'Selling up?'

He nodded.

'Obviously we'd be interested as buyers. LoPrice is a growing company and the Weale-On-Sea branch has been doing well lately. But we're struggling for space so taking over this property would be perfect for us.'

'Hang on a minute. What gave you the idea that my mum and dad were selling up?'

He seemed surprised by the question.

'It's what people are saying.'

'What people?'

He frowned.

'People generally. Just yesterday there was a couple in the store talking about what happened to your dad. Apparently, they were in All And Sundry when he had his heart attack and the ambulance came.'

'And they told you that the shop was going to close?'

'I suppose they were just speculating. But I think it's been clear for a while that the business has been struggling. And if your father has health issues on top of that …'

Annoyance began to well up inside Penny.

'So you think that the obvious solution would be for Mum and Dad to sell up?'

He smiled.

'Maisie and Bill deserve a long and happy retirement after all their hard work over the years.'

'So that LoPrice can flatten the shop and expand?'

'Obviously it's early days, but wouldn't that suit both parties?'

Something inside Penny seemed to pop.

'It might all seem obvious to you but it certainly isn't to me — or to my mum and dad. All And Sundry has been closed for the past two days because of what happened to Dad. But it will be opening again today and it will be staying open for the foreseeable future. I hope that's clear.'

His eyes had flashed at the sharp tone in her voice and his cheeks became tinged with red. When he spoke, it was with exaggerated calm.

'Very clear. Thank you for explaining your position. You're obviously busy so I won't bother you any longer. It's been a pleasure to meet you. Good day.'

He turned on his heels and strode off along the pavement. As Penny watched, he flicked his hand out and checked the time.

Her mouth curled. There was something very irritating about him, patronising even.

She looked at her own watch. But it

had stopped.

'Oh, for goodness sake,' she muttered.

She made her way to the front of the shop. A kindly-faced woman was standing there. She had been watching Penny's encounter with Graham Fraser in wide-eyed silence.

'Oh, Miss Penny, I'm that glad to see you. I was worried that you weren't going to turn up and then what would I have done?'

Penny enveloped her in a hug.

For as long as she could remember, Flo had been an essential part of All And Sundry.

She was a gem of a person.

'It's good to see you again, too, Flo.'

Flo rubbed a tear from her cheek.

'Your poor dad. I keep picturing him lying here on the pavement.'

Penny gave her a gentle squeeze.

'Don't worry, Dad is well on the mend. Maybe I could take you round to the hospital tonight so that you can see him for yourself. Would you like that?'

'That would be lovely, Miss Penny.

Thank you.'

She looked at Penny for a moment.

'So you're going to be looking after the shop while your dad recovers?'

'Not just me, Flo — me and you. The two of us are going to make a brilliant team.'

She took the keys from her pocket and found the one for the shop door.

'Now, let's get started. It's time we got All And Sundry back in business.'

Down to Business

Bill had always been the driving force behind All And Sundry. Maisie had just followed in his wake, doing her best to support him and to tidy up behind him. Over the years, he'd had all kinds of wonderful ideas for transforming the business.

Unfortunately, none of them had worked out quite as he had hoped. There was the time he had gone into renting videos — just as everyone started watching DVDs.

One summer, he turned an area of the shop over to a young beautician for painting people's nails. But her startling and unusual techniques had led to a whole series of complaints.

For a while he had kept cycles for hire at the back of the shop. That had been quite successful until some men hired them all for a group day out. They promptly disappeared along with the bikes and when Bill tried to cash their deposit cheque the bank pointed out that it was signed *Mr M Mouse*.

Bill's enthusiasm for the business was boundless but, for quite a number of years, All And Sundry had struggled to make Penny's parents much of a living.

Flo opened the window shutters and light flooded into the shop.

Penny looked around. The place really did seem a bit shabby. There were cracks on the tiled floor, the wallpaper was starting to peel and the woodwork could definitely do with a repaint.

Her eye was caught by some plastic footballs hanging in a net beside the till. They were on special offer at £1 each.

Penny frowned.

'Hang on, these are from the London Olympics!'

Flo nodded.

'Your dad got a whole bunch of them at a reduced price.'

'I'm not surprised. They're years out of date.'

'There's lots more in the storeroom

out the back. They sell quite well. Families like to have a ball to play with on the beach.'

She and Flo carried two small tables on to the pavement outside and placed some chairs round them. Their little café consisted of two tables outside and two more tables inside.

It wasn't a lot, but, then, their café didn't have much in the way of a menu, just tea and coffee, with cake when it was available.

All And Sundry didn't exactly have Starbucks shaking in its shoes.

'What's your normal routine, Flo?'

Flo puffed out her cheeks.

'I serve on the till, fill the shelves, clear the tables. Whatever needs doing, really.

Sometimes, if we're quiet, your mum gets me to go out back and bake some cakes to go with the teas and coffees.'

'I remember your cakes. Completely dreamy.'

Flo's cheeks flushed with pleasure.

'Oh, Miss Penny.'

'I'll tell you what — you keep an eye

on things in here for the moment while I have a go at the windows. Dad was right, they do need a wash.'

Flo's eyes widened.

'You be careful, Miss Penny. We don't want another accident.'

Penny smiled.

'Don't worry, Flo. I'll manage without the ladder.'

Penny went outside with a bucket of soapy water and a sponge and began to wipe down the windows.

There were plenty of people around. The pavements were filled with holiday-makers and she could see a steady stream of shoppers going in and out of LoPrice.

However no-one seemed very interested in what All And Sundry had to offer.

She looked through the bubbles at the window display inside, not that it could really be called a window display. There were some fluorescent buckets and spades on one side and two cardboard boxes of second-hand books on the other.

Stuck inside the windows were a few out-of-date posters for local events. It wasn't exactly eye-catching.

She cleared away the bubbles. It was all very well having the glass gleaming and bright, but what they needed was something eye-catching in the window to draw passers-by into the shop.

She went back inside, looking around for inspiration.

Flo was selling a can of cola to a young boy, their first customer of the day. He counted some coins carefully on to the counter.

Penny glanced round the shop for something else that he might like to buy.

Her eyes lit on the plastic footballs and she pulled one out of the bag.

'How about a football to go with your drink?'

The boy glanced at the price and then at his remaining coins. He shook his head.

'I don't have enough money, miss.'

Penny bounced the ball off the tiled floor and caught it in one hand.

'I'll sell it to you for twenty-five pence.'

His eyes widened. He looked again at the coins in his hand and then at Penny.

'Twenty-five pence?'

Penny nodded.

'It's a deal.'

He had just enough money. He handed the coins over to Flo and raced outside to his parents.

'Mum, Dad, I got this football for twenty-five pence!' There was no hiding his excitement.

Penny thought to herself for a moment.

'How many of these footballs are there out the back?'

Flo shrugged.

'I'm not sure exactly, hundreds probably. Your dad bought them from a chap who turned up in a van one day. It was filled with bags of the balls. Your dad reckoned he'd made a good deal, though your mum was always complaining about them making the storeroom even more cluttered than it already was.'

'I've had an idea, Flo. Go and fetch them.'

'What — all of them?'

'Yup. They're going to be our new window display.'

It didn't take long for Penny to clear the area inside the window and remove the old posters. Then, with Flo's help, she filled the space with the footballs.

Flo had been right, there were hundreds of the balls, all in net bags, and once they were packed into the shop window they almost reached the ceiling.

Leaving Flo to deal with the occasional customer, Penny started to make a poster.

She found some old marker pens in a drawer and wrote on a large piece of wrapping paper.

Olympic Footballs, 25p each — One Day Only!

She drew colourful stars round the wording and added a few simple drawings of people throwing balls at each other.

She was quite pleased with the result, especially the drawing of a little dog bouncing a ball off its head.

But Flo looked at the poster uncertainly.

'That's a lot cheaper than your dad was selling the footballs for, Miss Penny.'

'We need to get people into the shop, Flo, and this is going to do it.' Though as she spoke, Penny felt herself crossing her fingers.

However, the poster and the window display quickly began to attract attention from passers-by. Over the next hour or so, the footballs drew in a steady stream of customers.

For most of the customers, a football was all they wanted. But some, once they were in the shop, had a look around to see what else was on offer and bought some other bits and pieces.

There were a few customers wanting teas and coffees. Some of them even asked about cake. However, there was none available apart from what was left over from when the shop had closed and that was definitely past its use-by date.

At one point, as Penny dropped some

coins into the till, Flo looked at her in amazement.

'This is great, Miss Penny! It's ages since I've seen so many people coming into the shop.'

Penny just winked.

'Get used to it, Flo. This is how I want it all the time from now on.'

One of the customers looking for a football surprised her — it was a young man wearing a green LoPrice uniform.

'Don't you sell footballs in LoPrice?' she said, curious. 'I'm sure I saw some in that display of beach toys by your entrance.'

His cheeks flushed slightly but he didn't respond to her question.

'That's twenty-five pence, isn't it?'

'It is indeed.'

He handed over the money and hurried away without another word. She looked after him, puzzled. It seemed a rather odd thing for him to have done.

But then she was distracted by another customer placing a football in front of her, this time along with a bucket and spade.

'How about a tea or coffee while you're here?' she suggested brightly. 'One of our tables on the pavement is free at the moment.'

She wasn't used to being a saleswoman but she was starting to get into the swing of it, even enjoy it.

At one point late in the morning, there was a brief lull when Penny and Flo had a few moments to themselves.

'Weren't you saying that Mum sometimes got you to bake cakes for the shop, Flo?'

She nodded.

'Normally, Bill and Maisie just bought some cheap cakes from LoPrice to sell with the teas and coffees. But if things were quiet, your mum would get me to do some baking. The customers seemed to prefer that.'

'Of course they did. I remember your cakes, they're scrummy. If you ever entered 'Bake Off' ...'

Flo's cheeks went pink with pleasure.

'I wouldn't go that far, Miss Penny.'

'Well, I would, and that's what I want you to do now. I'll look after the shop for a while if you go out the back and start baking up a storm. When we open tomorrow morning, it won't be cheap footballs drawing the customers into All And Sundry, it'll be your cakes.'

There were times over the next hour or so when Penny rather regretted her decision.

She could have done with an extra pair of hands.

However, busy though she was, she made a point of chatting to all the customers. It wasn't just to make them feel welcome, she also wanted to get an idea of what else the shop could be selling.

None of the customers were buying more than a few bits and bobs. It was great to be busy but she was sure the shop could be selling a more attractive range of products.

It was about mid-afternoon when Penny noticed the two men out on the pavement.

They had an official look about them with their suits and ties and they were gazing at the window display, talking quietly together.

They came into the shop and went straight over to the footballs. They picked one up and began examining it carefully.

'Hi, there,' Penny smiled. 'Can I help you?'

They held up identity cards. They were Trading Standards officers.

'You certainly can help us — by removing every one of these footballs from sale.'

Penny's mouth sagged open.

'What?'

A young girl carried a ball over to the counter.

'Can I buy this, please?'

One of the officers removed it gently from her hands.

'I'm sorry. These balls are no longer available.'

'I don't understand,' Penny protested. 'They've been really popular.'

'Could you tell us where you got them from?'

'My father bought them from a salesman.'

'Perhaps we could speak to your father?'

Penny explained about his heart attack and how she had temporarily taken over the running of the shop.

'These balls have been on sale in the shop for ages. There hasn't been any problem up till now.'

The officer with the ball held it out for her to see.

'This isn't official Olympic merchandise.

It's using the Olympic logo but without authority. Selling goods like this is a serious offence.'

Penny gazed at him in shock.

'I had no idea – and I'm sure that my father didn't, either.'

The two men moved off to the side and spoke quietly together for a few moments.

They turned back to Penny.

'In the circumstances of your father's illness, we're not going to take this any further.'

40

Relief washed through Penny.

'Thank you so much.'

'However, we will have to confiscate the merchandise.'

'Confiscate it?'

'Absolutely. And I would advise your father to be a lot more careful about who he buys from in future. He needs to make sure that they're reputable suppliers.'

Penny watched in dismay as the officers gathered every one of the remaining footballs and took them to their van outside.

Then, having given Penny a receipt, they said their goodbyes.

She watched the van disappear round the corner. She felt suddenly weary and disappointed. Things had been going so well.

She looked at the shop window, empty now apart from the poster for footballs which were no longer available. With a mutter of frustration, she pulled it down.

Then, as she turned back into the shop, she noticed someone standing by the entrance to LoPrice. It was Graham Fraser.

He seemed to have been watching what was happening.

Suddenly, she remembered the LoPrice employee who had bought a football earlier.

Her eyes widened.

'He must have been told to do that so that they could check the football,' she muttered.

It must have been LoPrice who had tipped off the Trading Standards officers.

A rush of anger went through her as she watched the assistant manager disappear back into the supermarket. He had pretended to be so friendly and neighbourly, offering LoPrice's help with whatever was needed.

Instead, they had deliberately tried to get All And Sundry into trouble.

Cake, Anyone?

'Make sure that the alarm is set whenever you lock up. And don't forget the bins — they need to go out every Thursday night.'

'Dad, stop worrying. I'll be fine.'

Penny helped her father into the front seat of the car.

She hadn't said anything to him about the visit of the Trading Standards officers the day before. It would only have worried him.

She began to fix his seat belt but he waved her hand away irritably.

'I can manage. I'm not a complete basket case.'

Stifling a grin, Penny gave him an affectionate kiss on the cheek. His grumpiness suggested that he was getting back to his normal self.

Bill looked up at her.

'Maybe I should phone you once a day to check that everything is all right with the shop.'

'You'll do no such thing,' Maisie retorted. 'We're staying with May so that you can get some rest and relaxation, not to spend your time getting stressed about the shop.'

'Don't worry, Mum,' Penny murmured, giving Maisie a heartfelt hug. 'I'll look after All And Sundry. You concentrate on making sure that Dad gets better.'

'Everyone ready?' Auntie May called out.

Penny mouthed a thank-you at her and she gave a wink and a wave.

'The Lake District, here we come.'

A feeling of relief washed over Penny as she watched the car disappear round the corner.

Auntie May was such a sensible person.

She and Maisie between them would ensure that, over the next few weeks, Bill was set firmly on the road to recovery.

She glanced at her watch – time to get down to All And Sundry and open up.

'Flo, this is amazing.'

Flo's cheeks flushed at the praise.

'I've done a lemon drizzle, a Victoria sponge, a chocolate gateau and a slab of banana cake. I also did a tray of short-bread fingers and some flapjacks.'

Penny gave her a fierce hug.

'You're such a star. We need to find ways to get customers into the shop and I reckon this will do it.'

They carefully placed the cakes and biscuits under a glass stand.

'They look so delicious,' Penny murmured. Then her eyes narrowed.

'Though could you cut a slice out of each of the cakes?'

Flo smiled.

'Are you going to have a taste test?'

Penny shook her head.

'It just looks better that way. If a cake hasn't been started, the customers might think that no-one wants to eat it.'

Flo nodded.

'That makes sense.'

'Anyway, every crumb of those cakes and biscuits is going to be working at turning passers-by into customers – not at feeding me. Could you open up the shop, Flo? I want to make a poster.'

Flo grinned.

'Another one?'

'Let's hope this one is a bit more successful.'

It wasn't long before all four of All And Sundry's tables were occupied. The cakes and biscuits were selling well and Penny had sent Flo off to the kitchen to start baking again for all she was worth.

Earlier, Penny had placed a sandwich board out on the pavement and it was doing a fine job of attracting customers with its message.

TODAY'S SPECIAL: Cuppa & Cake — £1.75 only.

There were plenty of holidaymakers out and about on the streets and the chance to have a sit down with a cup of tea or coffee and a slice of Flo's cake was proving a draw.

Also attracting interest was the 'The

Cake Race' poster which Penny had stuck up on the wall by the door. It showed how many slices of each cake had been sold.

So far, it was a tie between the lemon drizzle and the chocolate gateau, though the banana cake was closing up fast.

Penny rang up the bill for a young couple with a toddler. They had bought a plastic bucket and spade for the little girl, who was clutching them eagerly.

Penny leaned over the counter with a smile.

'I hope you find some hidden treasure.'

The girl's eyes widened. 'When I was your age, my mum and dad told me that pirates had once visited Weale-On-Sea and left their treasure buried somewhere in the sand.'

The girl's mum smiled.

'Did you hear that, Tilly? We'd better get down to the beach quickly and start digging before someone else finds the treasure.'

'Can we take a picture of you?' the

dad asked, pulling out his phone. 'We're keeping a record of our holiday to go on the family blog.'

'Of course.' Penny nodded, then her eyes narrowed thoughtfully. 'How about taking the photo outside — then you can fit in the All And Sundry sign?'

'Good idea.'

Penny and the mum, with Tilly between them, stood by the shop doorway while the dad took a couple of photos. Then Penny in her turn took a picture of the family.

She handed back the phone.

'Thanks very much.' The dad smiled. 'Has All And Sundry got a website? We could send you copies of the photos to put on it.'

'It doesn't at the moment,' Penny replied, though her mind was suddenly racing.

A website for the shop would be a great idea.

'I would love copies of the photos, though. Let me give you my e-mail address.'

She stood for a moment watching the family heading eagerly off to the beach.

All kinds of ideas were flickering through her head, thoughts about how she might build up All And Sundry's presence on social media — its own blog maybe, a Twitter feed, a Facebook page.

Her mind began to churn with possibilities.

There was the sound of a throat clearing next to her.

'Hello — anyone at home?'

Penny snapped out of her daydream. All at once, a broad smile spread across her face. Standing there were two very familiar faces.

'Brian, Eric!'

She gave them both a delighted hug. The two men had been regular customers at All And Sundry for as long as she could remember. They came in together almost every day to read their morning papers over a cup of tea.

After they'd discussed the main stories at great length with each other and anyone else who would listen, they had a

long and argumentative game of dominoes. They never had anything else apart
from their cup of tea and they managed
to make it last for at least a couple of
hours.

'Don't tell me — two strong teas, one
with sugar?' Penny smiled, knowing
what the answer would be. 'And how
about a couple of Flo's flapjacks to go
with them?'

Brian looked at her with a disapprov-
ing frown.

'Just the teas, please.'

'Has your dad left yet, Penny?' Eric
asked. 'We went round to see him yesterday and he said he was being dragged
off to the Lake District.'

Penny laughed.

'He left this morning, still complaining like mad. Mum and Auntie May are
determined to make him relax over the
next few weeks but he's not very keen on
the idea.'

'You send him and Maisie our best
wishes when you speak to them next.'

Penny smiled.

'I will. Now, let me get those teas.'

Brian was looking round with a frown.

'You're a bit busy today.' He made it sound like a complaint.

Penny nodded.

'It's Flo's cakes. We've got them on special offer and the customers can't get enough of them. You really should give them a try.'

He ignored the suggestion.

'But where are we going to sit? There was always a free table when your mum and dad were looking after the shop. We're your oldest customers.'

He gazed in suspicion at the people chatting and laughing. Penny had a feeling that he was expecting her to clear the customers from one of the tables so that he and Eric could enjoy their cups of tea in peace.

She looked around. If they'd had a few more tables, they could easily have filled them. The special offer was attracting plenty of passers-by.

She suddenly thought of the waste ground at the side of the café. It was in a bit of a rough state but there was lots of room there and it did have a great view of the beach and the bay.

She hurried round from behind the counter.

'I've just had a thought, Brian. Back in a tick.'

She hurried through to the storeroom.

There were delicious smells wafting from the kitchen.

'How's it going, Flo?' she called in passing.

'Yes, fine.' Flo suddenly stuck her head out of the kitchen door, her hands covered in flour. 'Hang on, who's looking after the shop?'

'Don't worry — this won't take a second.'

The storeroom was packed with all kinds of items which had gradually accumulated over the years. Penny had had a quick look at it the day before and she remembered seeing some deckchairs leaning against a wall. They weren't new and Penny wasn't sure why they were there but they were just what she needed.

She grabbed a couple and returned to the café.

'Here you go, chaps. You can sit outside on these while you have your tea and enjoy the view.'

'Deckchairs?' Brian clearly didn't approve.

Eric clapped him on the shoulder.

'Stop being an old stick-in-the-mud. They'll be fine.' He helped Penny set them up and settled himself into one. 'Perfect.'

He smiled.

'But where are we going to put our domino set?' Brian complained.

Penny thought for a moment and then hurried back into the shop. She came back with an empty cardboard box, turned it upside down and set it on the ground between the two chairs. She tested its stability.

'Yup, that will do as a table. I'll be back with your teas in a second, gents.'

She hurried off before Brian could give vent to the obvious disapproval on his face.

Things didn't slacken off at all throughout the day. There was a steady stream of customers drawn by the special offer.

When she had a moment, Penny brought out the rest of the deckchairs and left them leaning against the wall.

The next time she went outside, they were all set up and in use. They seemed particularly popular with family groups.

While the parents relaxed over their cuppas, the children ran around enjoying themselves.

'What a view!' A middle-aged couple smiled as they tucked into their slices of cake. 'You are so lucky.'

Penny looked around. It was true. The waste ground might be rather rough and unkempt but it had a perfect view of the beach and the bay beyond.

It occurred to her that they really should be making better use of it.

'Well, that was a busy day!' Flo gasped as the last customer left and they closed up the shop.

Penny gave a weary sigh.

'You can say that again. I don't think I stopped from the moment we opened this morning.' She put a hand on Flo's arm.

'You've been such a star. I was constantly thinking that we were about to run out of cakes and biscuits but somehow you kept them coming.'

Flo shrugged.

'It wasn't a problem because that was all I had to do. It was you I felt so sorry for, Miss Penny. You had to cope with everything else all by yourself.'

Penny grinned.

'Being run off your feet is a nice problem to have.'

Penny went to collect the sandwich board from the pavement. She looked at her homemade *Special Offer* sign. On the spur of the moment, she picked it up and gave it a fervent kiss.

'Good job today.'

Then her eyes were caught by a figure up the road. It was Graham Fraser. He was changing the display outside LoPrice.

Her cheeks flushed at the thought of him seeing her kissing the sandwich board.

He raised a hand in greeting.

For a moment, Penny didn't respond. But then she decided that she was being silly and she held up her own hand.

She took the sandwich board inside and then returned to collect the tables and chairs. She noticed that Graham had been joined outside LoPrice by an older man. The two of them were talking together.

They glanced in her direction and Penny got the impression that they were discussing either her or All And Sundry. Flo came out to help.

'Do you know who that is, Flo — the older chap?' Penny asked.

Flo snorted.

'That's Howard France. He's the manager of LoPrice and he's a right grumpy one, too. I don't think I've ever seen him with a smile on his face.'

Once everything was inside, Penny closed the doors.

'You can go now, Flo, I'll sort everything else out. And thanks for your help today. I couldn't have done it without you.'

After a quick hug, Flo left and Penny locked up. It was another hour or so before she herself left. She'd had to tally up the accounts for the day and make a list of ingredients to buy at the cash-and-carry for Flo's cakes.

However, she also took the opportunity to have a good look at the storeroom. It was jam-packed with a hotchpotch of different things.

On one shelf alone she found artificial flowers, jigsaws of famous places, ukeleles in boxes and sporting gnomes.

She brought a selection out into the shop and spread them around any spaces she could find on the shelves. The more items the customers had to spend their money on the better.

She locked up the shop, making sure that she had set the alarm.

She felt exhausted but satisfied. They hadn't made a fortune on her first couple of days in charge but at least All And Sundry had been busy.

The next challenge was to build on that.

She wandered past LoPrice, which was still open, wondering if there was anything at home to have for her tea. But then she suddenly stopped in shock.

In the window there was a large poster. It was new — it certainly hadn't been there that morning.

Café Special: Drink & Cake £1.50. Plenty of seating available.

Penny gazed at the poster in disbelief, a surge of anger boiling up inside her.

She strode into the shop. There were a few customers dotted here and there but it wasn't particularly busy.

Graham Fraser was sitting at one of the tills and he smiled as he spotted her.

However, the expression on his face faltered as she approached.

Penny pointed at the poster in the window.

'Is that really necessary?'

He flushed.

'I'm not sure what you mean.'

'The very day we put on a special offer in our shop to drum up a bit of business, you immediately undercut us.'

He shrugged uncomfortably.

'It has nothing to do with All And Sundry.

We often put on special offers for our customers.'

'Oh, come on,' Penny retorted. 'I wasn't born yesterday.'

'Is there a problem here?'

It was Howard France, the manager. He was approaching with a frown.

'There certainly is a problem,' Penny retorted. 'I'm doing my best to keep All And Sundry going while my dad recovers from his illness and you seem determined to make things difficult for us.'

'The special offer in our café has coincided with one at All And Sundry,'

Graham Fraser explained.

'It's no coincidence,' Penny retorted.

Howard France looked at her coldly.

'The pricing policy at LoPrice is nothing to do with anyone else. If you can't compete with us, then that's tough. All's fair in love and business.'

He turned on his heel and strode off.

Penny gazed at Graham Fraser, her eyes blazing.

War is Declared!

'He just can't be trusted, Angela. One moment he's all smiles, the next he and that boss of his are stabbing you in the back.'

'You make it sound very dramatic.'

Penny was sitting up in bed wrapped in her duvet.

It was so good to hear the sound of Angela's voice. She'd missed her friend.

'Are you sure there isn't a little bit of potential romance lingering somewhere in the background?'

Penny hooted with laughter, almost spilling the glass of wine in her hand.

'Graham Fraser is the last person in the world I'd be interested in romantically.'

'Yet you seem to have spent most of the phone call talking about him.'

'I've been talking about him because he's being such a pain. All I want is for All And Sundry to survive until Mum and Dad get back. But he and his boss seem determined to make things as hard as possible for us.'

'I notice that you've avoided any mention of his appearance so far. Let me guess — he's not a wrinkly, middle-aged man with bad skin and terrible hair.'

'I suppose he is quite good-looking in a conventional sort of way,' Penny admitted.

She hurried on as Angela yelled triumphantly in the background.

'But that's not the point. A little shop like All And Sundry isn't any sort of threat to LoPrice. Yet it's almost as if they're desperate to put us out of business.'

'Well, the Penny I know isn't going to allow that to happen.'

'You're right there. I'm not sure how long Mum and Dad are going to be away, but when they return All And Sundry will be thriving.'

'That's my girl.'

'Anyway, enough about me. I can't believe that you've decided not to go to

Europe at all this summer.'

Angela made a dismissive noise.

'The whole point of the holiday was for us to have a good time together. It wouldn't be the same if I went by myself.'

'But surely you could get someone else to go with you?'

'Come on, Penny, there's no way I could find a replacement for you, not an acceptable one, anyway.'

Penny felt herself smiling.

'That's a nice thing to say.'

'Everyone else is far too sensible.'

'You cheeky thing!'

'It's the truth, ma'am, nothing but the truth.'

'So what are you going to do over the summer instead?'

'I'm not sure yet but I'll think of something. Hey, look at the time, I'd better go. You need your beauty sleep if you're going to put that hunk from LoPrice back in his box tomorrow.'

'He's not a hunk. At least not to me.'

Angela just laughed.

'Speak to you soon, Penny.'

Penny felt in surprisingly good spirits as she strode along the promenade the next morning. It wasn't just that Angela's phone call had cheered her up, she had also come up with a corker of an idea.

As she passed LoPrice, she stopped for a moment and gazed at the Special Offer poster in the window.

Like all of LoPrice's posters, it was printed with the company logo and a flashy design, a stark contrast to her hand-drawn efforts.

But Penny decided that she preferred her own.

'Much more individual,' she muttered.

She could see Graham Fraser inside the shop putting some tins on a shelf. He spotted her and looked at her uncertainly for a moment.

Penny put on her brightest smile and waved at him cheerfully. The surprise on his face almost made her laugh out loud as she turned and headed off to All And Sundry.

He wasn't the only one who could be a puzzle to understand.

Her eyes narrowed. And LoPrice wasn't the only business which could show a competitive spirit.

Flo was already waiting at All And Sundry.

'That's what I like to see, an eager worker,' Penny smiled as she opened up.

But Flo's face was wreathed in concern.

'Did you see the sign in LoPrice's window?'

Penny nodded.

'I noticed it last night.'

Flo's eyes flashed with anger.

'It's just because we were attracting lots of customers yesterday. It's so unfair. They think that because they're a big organisation they can just squash us like … like an irritating fly.'

Penny grinned.

'Don't worry, Flo. They're about to discover that this irritating fly has turned into an angry wasp.'

Penny unlocked the door and let them

into the shop.

'LoPrice may be big but they don't have all the advantages. For a start, their café is inside the shop — it's all noise and bustle there. If you wanted to go somewhere for a cuppa, would that be your first choice?'

She nodded towards the beach.

It was a gorgeous morning with a few fluffy white clouds dotted across the blue sky, holidaymakers wandering here and there on the golden sand, the sound of seagulls in the background.

'Especially when you had somewhere with a view like this just down the road,' Penny added.

Flo nodded slowly.

'Most people would prefer to come here.'

'Exactly. We have a fantastic view to offer and … ' Penny put an arm round Flo's shoulders '… we have something that LoPrice just can't match, and that's you making our cakes.'

Flo flushed at the praise.

'Talking of which, how are our cake

supplies doing?'

'We have more than enough at the moment, thanks to me being able to spend all day on it yesterday. There's Black Forest gateau, stem ginger loaf, banana bread, lemon sponge . . . oh, all kinds of things.

And I've also done some special biscuits for the children.'

'Sounds fantastic.'

Flo looked at her uncertainly.

'I'm just worried that, if everyone goes to LoPrice for their cuppas, we'll be left with all this cake and no-one to buy it.'

Penny winked.

'Leave it to me. Could you look after the shop for ten minutes or so? I have a poster to make — another one.'

Penny pinned blank sheets of paper to both sides of the sandwich board and wrote in colourful lettering.

TODAY'S SPECIAL. 20% discount in our café for all LoPrice shoppers — just show your receipt.

She wasn't particularly artistic but she

managed to include some cups, cakes and biscuits as decorations around the words.

Then, as an afterthought, she added large hearts at the bottom containing the message *With love from All And Sundry*.

She stood back and gazed at it critically for a moment.

'That's not bad. Have a look at this, Flo,' she called.

Flo's eyes widened as she read the poster.

'Can you do that?'

'What?'

'Give a discount to customers from another shop?'

Penny shrugged.

'I don't see why not. People who shop at LoPrice go there because it's cheap. They'll be keen on a bargain, so I reckon they'll be very interested when they see this sign.'

She carried the sandwich board to the street outside.

'Anyway, we'll soon find out.'

She set out the deckchairs on the waste

ground as she had done the day before.

She included cardboard boxes to use as tables but this time she covered them with some cloths she had brought from home so that they looked a bit more presentable.

'Though maybe posies of flowers on the tables might be nice, too,' she murmured to herself thoughtfully.

She mentally added it to her list of possible ideas for All And Sundry and grinned. The list was getting longer all the time.

She took a moment to stand back and look at the effect. The deckchairs and informal tables had a relaxed and cheery appearance. However, the waste ground wasn't exactly beautiful.

There wasn't much she could do there and then about the rubble and clumps of weed but at least she could clear up some of the smaller items of rubbish – when she had a few minutes to spare.

She smiled to herself ruefully and added that job to the list as well.

When she went back into the shop, she

found the two old friends already there.

'Brian, Eric — our first customers of the day.'

'Morning, Penny,' they responded in unison.

They had been served by Flo and they were both reading their papers with their mugs of tea close at hand. They had clearly decided that if they wanted to make sure of a table at All And Sundry then they needed to arrive early.

Flo was gazing at them in disapproval.

'Those two old rascals will be there for the rest of the morning,' she muttered.

'They won't buy anything apart from those cups of tea and there'll be lots of other customers desperate for a table.'

Penny smiled.

'Brian and Eric have been coming to this shop for as long as anyone can remember. As far as I'm concerned, they can sit at their table for as long as they like.

'But never mind that, Flo, I've got something for you to do. Do you have your cake knife handy?'

A few minutes later, Penny was setting out a little table on the pavement by the entrance to the shop. On it, she arranged a selection of bowls containing nibble-sized samples of all the cakes which were available to buy that day. In front of the bowls were labels showing the names of the cakes and each bowl was protected by a transparent cover.

'What's that you're doing out there, Penny?' Brian called from inside the shop.

'Try-Before-You-Taste, Brian,' Penny retorted. 'There are some free samples of Flo's cakes here so that you can decide which one you like best before you order a slice.'

She looked at the bowls thoughtfully.

Then picking up the one containing nibbles of the stem ginger cake, she carried it into the shop.

'Come on, Brian, have a taste.'

He waved his hand at her.

'We don't want cake. We're happy with our cups of tea.'

Penny offered the bowl to Eric. He

hesitated for a moment but then took a sample. He popped it into his mouth and his eyes widened.

'Now, that's really nice.'

Penny grinned.

'Well, if you want some more, you know what to do.'

All And Sundry was busy throughout the morning with a number of customers coming in with LoPrice receipts and claiming their discount. At one point, Penny noticed to her amusement that Eric was tucking into a slice of ginger cake while Brian glared at him with obvious disapproval.

Then, during a quiet moment, Flo came over to where Penny was standing by the till. 'I've had an idea,' she said uncertainly. 'You probably think it's stupid …'

'Don't be daft. What is it?'

'I was using an icing bag earlier to decorate the lemon sponge and there's some icing left in it.'

'And?'

'Well, just to use it up I thought that,

72

if any children bought one of our biscuits, we could add their names written
in icing.'

Penny gazed at her and, after a
moment, Flo shook her head and turned
away.

'No, it was a silly idea.'

'Silly? It's genius!' Penny grasped her
by the shoulders. 'The children will love
it.'

Soon another poster had gone up, and
it was just as she had hoped. When children were offered the option of having
their names written on their biscuits,
they leaped at the opportunity.

Even some of the parents asked for it,
too.

Penny made her way through the café.
It was filled with chatter and laughter.
To her amusement, Brian and Eric had
been joined by two other customers and
the four of them were gazing with deeply
serious expressions at the dominoes
spread out in front of them.

She went out on to the pavement.

'Are you finished?' she asked a family

group getting up from their table.

'Yes, thanks. The cake was dreamy,' the mother said.

'Now we're off to the beach again!' The little girl was jumping around with excitement.

'Have a good time.'

As Penny wiped down the table, she noticed Graham with Howard France standing outside LoPrice.

She smiled to herself and wondered if they were discussing the discount available to LoPrice customers.

The two men were talking in an animated manner and Howard France in particular didn't seem very happy.

It was no surprise to Penny when, a few minutes later, she noticed Graham standing on the pavement outside All And Sundry gazing at the sandwich board.

Feeling curious, she went to join him.

'Can I help you?'

Graham looked at her hesitantly for a moment. He didn't seem quite sure how to start.

However, Penny was in no mood to

put him at his ease and she just waited until he finally broke the silence between them.

'It's this sign,' he said, pointing to the sandwich board. 'Mr France insists that you remove it at once.'

Penny gazed around.

'I don't see Mr France anywhere. If he has a message, can't he give it to me himself?'

Graham flushed slightly.

'He's rather busy. He asked me to speak to you.'

'I'm busy, too. So you can tell him that I have no intention of removing the sign.'

She decided to twist the knife in the wound just a little.

'And you can add that it's been very successful. It's brought lots of LoPrice customers into the shop today.'

His eyes flickered.

'But you're using the LoPrice name to advertise your own shop. It doesn't seem right.'

Penny just gazed at him. There were crinkles at the corners of his eyes as if he was used to smiling.

However, he wasn't smiling now.

'Perhaps I can remind you of what I was told yesterday — all is fair in love and business. Now, if you don't mind, I have work to do.'

Turning on her heels, she went back into the shop. It wasn't until she had reached the counter that she glanced round. But he was gone.

★ ★ ★

'It was brilliant, Angela,' Penny said down the phone that evening. 'There was nothing he could say.'

Angela laughed.

'I expect he was struck dumb with excitement at being right next to his one true love.'

'Will you stop that?' Penny protested.

'Graham Fraser is as uninterested in me as I am with him. We don't think of each other in that way at all.'

'Hmm,' Angela murmured. She didn't seem convinced.

Oh, Yowza!

'The biscuits with the children's names on them are selling really well. Sometimes the children like them so much they prefer to keep them rather than eat them,' Flo said.

Penny laughed ruefully.

'With a bit more practice, when I write the names with the icing, they might even become recognisable.'

She and Flo gazed at the computer screen. Penny was keeping a record on a spreadsheet of how many slices of the different cakes they sold each day and how the customers had rated them.

Flo frowned.

'I was surprised the coffee and walnut cake didn't sell better yesterday. The customers who chose it really liked it.'

Penny nodded.

'It got our highest rating. Maybe next time you make it, we'll hand round lots of free samples. Once people have a taste, they won't be able to resist it. Anyway, do you know what you're going to bake today?'

Flo held up a piece of paper covered in scribbles.

'I've got my list.'

The two of them had decided to change the selection of cakes every day so that there was always something new to choose from. In fact, that had given Penny an idea and she had started a Cake Club for regular customers. If they bought six different slices of cake, they got the seventh for free.

The scheme had already attracted quite a bit of interest with some customers visiting the café almost every day and getting their Cake Club cards stamped.

Flo got to her feet.

'OK, I'll get off and start baking.'

'And I'll open up the shop. Another day, another dollar.'

It was a week since Penny had taken over the running of All And Sundry and she and Flo were gradually settling into a routine.

They always got together first thing to plan the day. Then Flo spent the mornings baking up a storm in the kitchen while Penny looked after the shop.

And in the afternoons, while Flo took care of the customers, Penny worked on her plans for developing All And Sundry.

Penny smiled to herself. She was so full of ideas. The notebook in her back pocket was filled with scribbles.

Of course, some ideas were more practical than others. Just the night before while lying in bed, she had suddenly pictured a whole wall of the shop covered with signed photos of the celebrities who often visited Weale-On-Sea to give concerts and shows. That might take a while to sort out.

On the other hand, encouraging customers to take selfies of themselves with the All And Sundry sign in the background and posting them on social media might be easier to organise. She hoped to get started on that straightaway.

The bell above the door sounded.

'Brian, Eric — our first customers again.'

She smiled to herself. She would get started on the idea just as soon as she had a spare moment, which might be a while.

It was a busy morning in the shop. As soon as a table became free, someone else occupied it.

The deckchairs on the waste ground were again proving popular and, whenever Penny went outside, some sort of game was going on — people throwing a frisbee or kicking a ball around.

Someone started blowing bubbles and, within moments, there was a hubbub of children trying to burst them.

Penny was amused when Brian asked for a piece of Flo's chocolate and orange tray-bake to go with his cup of tea. He obviously hadn't been able to resist following Eric's example.

When he ordered it, Brian glared at her as if daring her to say something but, apart from the twinkle in her eyes, she didn't react.

It was in the early afternoon while Penny was busy washing some cups when her attention was caught by a tall, rangy figure standing in the doorway.

He gazed around, one hand on the guitar slung around his shoulder. He clearly wasn't a local. He had a golden tan with curly beach-blond hair tumbling round his ears.

His T-shirt hung loosely over his cut-off denims and Penny got the definite impression of a body that was used to working out.

She smiled to herself. The noise in the café had dropped slightly as some of the female customers suddenly found themselves rather distracted.

'Can I help?'

'A mug of tea, please. Good and strong, three sugars.'

'Don't tell me — you're from Australia.' The accent had seemed fairly clear.

His eyes flashed.

'That place? Nah, I'm from God's own country — New Zealand.'

'Sorry,' Penny apologised.

He grinned.

'No problems. I'm just travelling round Europe for the summer, having the time of my life … '

A pang went through Penny. If things had worked out differently, she might have been doing the very same thing.

She handed him his mug of tea with a smile. On the other hand, Weale-On-Sea did have its own attractions.

'Help yourself to milk and sugar.'

There were dishes to be washed and tables to be cleared but Penny didn't feel in any hurry to go off and deal with that just then.

She watched him spoon some sugar into his tea. She noticed that his finger-nails were clean and well cared for — she liked that in a man.

'Actually, I wanted to ask you a favour,' he said after a moment.

Penny leaned forward on the counter.

'I would love to do you a favour,' she murmured.

Her cheeks suddenly pinked as she realised what she had said. The words had come out without her thinking about them.

She stood up again hurriedly.

'What I mean is … '

But he had burst out laughing and, as their eyes met, Penny found herself joining in.She wondered if he would be sticking around Weale-On-Sea for a bit. She wouldn't mind getting to know him better.

He flicked the guitar strap round his shoulder.

'I do a bit of busking and I was wondering if I could try for a while outside your shop, where the deckchairs are.'

Penny smiled.

'Sure, feel free. I'm sure the customers will enjoy it.'

She had no idea how musical he was. But she thought that the customers would probably put up with his presence for a while no matter what sort of racket he made — the female ones anyway.

'That's brilliant.' He stuck his hand across the counter, the amber beads round his wrist clinking gently. 'The name's Jordy.'

'Penny,' she replied and his hand enveloped hers. It was a pleasant sensation and Penny didn't feel any urge to let go.

His mouth twitched in amusement. He recovered his hand and touched a finger to his forehead.

'Good to meet you, Penny. I'll go and get myself set up.'

She watched him stroll outside with his tea. Things were definitely looking up.

'I like that music,' Flo murmured when she appeared out of the kitchen some time later.

The baking was done for the day apart from some icing which needed to wait until the cakes had cooled down.

'It's not bad, is it? He's a chap called Jordy from New Zealand. He turned up earlier.'

The music had been drifting pleasantly into the shop for the past hour or so. Jordy had been playing a lot of summer hits. He had a warm voice and you could sense the smile in it as he was singing.

'Go and have a listen, Flo,' Penny suggested. 'See what you think.'

She returned a couple of minutes later.

'Goodness, he's nice.' There was a slightly distant look in her eyes.

'Now, Flo,' Penny said with a stern expression, 'remember that you're a happily married woman.'

A flush of red coloured Flo's cheeks.

'Oh, Miss Penny, you don't think … you can't believe … '

Penny burst out laughing and gave her a hug.

'Just joking. Though, if Jordy is typical of New Zealand, then I think I might need to go there on holiday some day soon.'

'Anyway, that's me done in the kitchen,' Flo said, eager to change the subject. 'I can take over from you now, if you like.'

'That would be great. There's something I want to sort out.'

Flo smiled.

'Don't tell me. You've had another idea.'

Penny grinned.

'Something like that.'

The day before, she had carefully chalked a large hashtag in front of the name on the shop's sign. If #AllAndSundry started getting mentioned here and there on social media then it would do the shop no harm at all.

She had also been thinking of ways to encourage customers to take selfies of themselves at the shop.

Then, looking through the storeroom, she had found the perfect solution; full-size cardboard cut-outs of different cinema stars from the past. She vaguely remembered them from the time her dad had run his short-lived video rental business, and had put the cut-outs out on the pavement as advertising.

They had been fairly tatty even then, and their condition hadn't been helped by spending the last few years at the back of the storeroom. However, they would be perfect for what Penny had in mind.

She picked up the cut-out of Luke Skywalker and looked at it thoughtfully.

Having flicked off a couple of spiders, she laid the cut-out down on a table in the storeroom and wiped it with a damp cloth.

'All I need now is a sharp knife and a steady hand.'

Twenty minutes later she was standing the cut-out on the pavement outside the shop.

Next to it she put a cut-out of Princess Leia and next to that a cut-out of R2D2, the robot. All three had blank circles where their faces had once been.

She crossed the road and had a look at the effect from there. She nodded in satisfaction.

'If that doesn't get people taking selfies with #AllAndSundry in the background then I don't know what will.'

Even as she walked back across the road, two children were vying to be first to put their faces in the R2D2 cut-out and their mother was about to take a photo of them.

She grinned to herself.

'Thanks, R2.'

Penny spent the next hour or so sorting out a new window display. She scattered some sand on the floor inside the window and set up a deckchair on it. She had no idea why there was a mannequin in the storeroom but soon it was sitting in the deckchair, wearing Penny's swimsuit, her sunglasses and a big floppy hat.

The mannequin was holding a camera in her hand and was aiming it at herself as if to take a photo.

There was a large poster in the window. *Send Us Your Selfies! #AllAndSundry.*

On the sand beside the deckchair Penny had placed an open laptop. Every few seconds a new picture appeared on its screen showing someone with the #AllAndSundry sign in the back-ground.

'Get to work,' she whispered to the mannequin. 'Go viral.'

Outside, on the waste ground, Jordy was singing the old Mungo Jerry classic, 'In The Summertime', and it seemed to be proving popular with the customers.

'How's it going?' she mouthed in passing as she collected the empty cups and plates from the tables.

He nodded towards the baseball cap lying upside on the ground in front of him. It contained a healthy collection of coins, even one or two notes. She gave him a thumbs-up sign.

Just then, she noticed Graham Fraser outside LoPrice pushing some trolleys back into line. He seemed to be watching them at the same time.

Afterwards, Penny wasn't sure why she did it, but Jordy had just come to the end of the song and as the customers cheered, she hurried over to him clapping enthusiastically and then wrapped her arms round him in a big hug.

The cheers became even louder and, with a grin, Jordy kissed her on the cheek. Penny let go of him, flushing slightly.

Graham was no longer there and she found herself feeling irritated and confused at herself. She wasn't sure what had impelled her to hug Jordy but now she wished that she hadn't.

But, all at once, everything else was driven from her mind. She had just spotted a very familiar figure standing by the entrance of the shop.

'Angela!' she cried in disbelief.

A chaotic few moments followed as they grabbed each other in a prolonged hug.

'It is so good to see you.' Penny grinned.

'But what are you doing here?'

Angela held out her hands.

'It suddenly occurred to me, if I can't go to Europe for the summer, why not go to the seaside instead?'

'You're going to spend the summer here?'

Angela nodded.

'That's the plan. It's been such fun hearing your phone-calls and about everything you're getting up to. But you seem so busy. It occurred to me that you might be able to do with some help?'

Penny's mouth fell open.

'We certainly could.' But then she grimaced. 'Oh, but we can't afford to take on a new employee. There just isn't the money.'

'I thought about that. How about if you put me up at your mum and dad's house and I do two or three hours in the shop each day in exchange?'

'That would be fantastic. We could certainly do with an extra pair of hands and it would be brilliant having you to stay. There's plenty of room.'

Angela smiled widely.

'Summer at the seaside — what could be better? And I could learn to surf — I've always wanted to surf!'

'Oh, Angela.' They wrapped their arms around each other again. 'It's going to be so good to have you here.'

Then Penny felt Angela's arms slacken. She stepped back.

Angela was gazing across the waste ground at where Jordy was about to start his next song.

'Oh, yowza,' she whispered. 'I want

one of those.'

There wasn't much doubt about it. She was taken with Jordy — and badly.

Surf's Up

Angela laughed.

'I must be getting better at it — I only fell off the surf-board twenty times this morning.'

She was busily washing some cups and plates in the sink while Penny sat at the till dealing with customers.

'Jordy reckons that once I've fallen off a thousand times then I can start calling myself a proper surfer. At this rate, it won't be too long.'

Penny smiled ruefully to herself. If she'd had any hopes with regard to Jordy, they were scuppered the moment that he and Angela met.

Penny hadn't really believed in love at first sight until then. But when she introduced the two of them, she could almost hear the fireworks going off — they hadn't been able to take their eyes off each other.

Jordy had decided to give the busking

a break for a bit and they had settled into a couple of free deckchairs and started chatting.

An hour later they were still chatting and the coffees Penny had brought for them had long since grown cold. They hadn't even touched Flo's cinnamon flapjacks.

At some point, Jordy had offered to show Angela around Weale-On-Sea and they had gone off for a wander. When they returned much later, Jordy's arm was tight round Angela's shoulders and Angela was cuddling up against him as if she wanted to stay there for the rest of her life.

That evening, Angela had seemed strangely uncertain as she and Penny made their way along the promenade to Bill and Maisie's house.

'You're such a good friend, I wouldn't want to spoil things for you. Were you hoping you and Jordy might, well … ?'

Penny burst out laughing.

'Any thoughts I might have had in that direction went out the window as soon as you and Jordy met. I've never seen anything like it.'

Angela didn't seem convinced.

'I can leave — I can get out of your way. Your friendship means so much to me that I wouldn't want to do anything to mess that up.'

Penny stopped and turned to her.

'Don't be daft, Angela. You and Jordy are perfect together, anyone can see that.'

Angela grabbed her in a hug.

'I do like Jordy,' Penny went on as they continued along the promenade arm-in-arm. 'I've only known him five minutes and already he feels like a friend, but it's nothing more than that. So good luck to the two of you.'

Angela gave her arm a squeeze and Penny grinned.

'Though if you come across any other blokes as gorgeous as him then just send them my way.'

Angela dried her hands on a towel while Penny rang up some groceries for a customer.

'I'll go and check the tables outside.'

Penny smiled.

'And tell that noisy bunch of surfers to turn the racket down a bit.'

Although Angela had only been in Weale-On-Sea for a few days, she hadn't wasted any time. She was very keen to learn to surf and with Jordy's help she had started going out on the water every day. He had learned to surf almost as soon as he could walk.

There was a thriving surfers' scene at Weale-On-Sea and Angela had quickly become involved in it. As a result, surfers had started dropping by All And Sundry on a regular basis. They added a lot of fun and laughter to the atmosphere.

Penny could hear a group of them now singing along with Jordy as he played some old Beach Boys classics.

Penny looked round the shop. The tables inside and out were full of customers and she knew that most of the deckchairs on the waste ground were taken up.

She had reorganised the groceries on the shelves and was now offering a selection of picnic snacks which people might want to take to the beach. They were turning out to be popular and she'd already had to increase her orders twice.

She had also come to an agreement with the bookshop in town. They had provided her with a couple of their rotating stands which were filled with a selection of gaudy bestsellers, lurid crime thrillers and torrid romances.

Again, they were proving popular with holidaymakers, especially those planning an uninterrupted laze on the beach. All And Sundry didn't make a huge amount from the sales, since the profits had to be shared with the bookshop. But they added to the variety of goods available at the shop and drew in a few more customers.

A young girl and her brother came hand-in-hand up to the till. Penny could see their parents watching encouragingly from the doorway with a poodle on a lead.

'Can we have some biscuits with our

names on them, please?' the girl asked, her eyes wide and hopeful.

Penny smiled.

'Of course you can. What are your names?'

'I'm Jenny,' the girl began.

'And I'm Tyrion,' her little brother squeaked.

'Now, those are two really lovely names,' Penny said, taking a couple of large round biscuits from a plastic container. 'I'll start with you, Tyrion.'

Squeezing the piping bag carefully, she got to work. At first, she had been terrible at writing the children's names on the biscuits. It was much harder than it looked and sometimes it had been almost impossible to make out what she had written. But with practice she was getting better at it.

She gazed at the biscuit critically and then nodded to herself. It was a perfectly respectable Tyrion. Then she wrote Jenny on the other biscuit.

'Would you like some sprinkles on them?'

They looked at each other for a moment and nodded eagerly. Then, as Penny handed over the biscuits, her eyes narrowed. She'd had a sudden thought.

'Is that your dog?'

'That's Napoleon,' Tyrion stated firmly.

'He's a pooble.'

'A poodle,' Jenny corrected him with a frown.

Penny leaned over the counter and whispered in a conspiratorial voice.

'Would you like me to do a biscuit for him, too? You can have it for free.'

Their eyes widened in amazement.

'Yes, please!' Jenny gasped.

Penny had to squash up the last few letters of Napoleon's name to make it fit.

But her dodgy writing didn't seem to spoil the children's excitement. They rushed out to their parents and showed them the biscuits eagerly.

'Thank you,' the mother mouthed as the father began taking photos of Jenny, Tyrion and Napoleon with their biscuits. Penny smiled to herself — a few more satisfied customers.

Flo appeared out of the back and made her way over to the till.

'That's all the baking finished for today, Miss Penny. I found a recipe for pear and ginger loaf on the internet. It's turned out really well.'

Penny's eyes widened.

'Sounds fantastic. Can I have a taste?'

'You wait till tomorrow,' Flo retorted.

Penny's eyes narrowed.

'Hang on, I'm in charge here at All And Sundry. And it's part of my job to taste everything before it goes on sale to make sure that it's up to the shop's high standards.'

Flo just gave her a look and Penny grinned ruefully.

'Oh, well, it was worth a try.'

'Anyway, shall I take over at the till now?' Flo asked.

Penny nodded.

'I'll check up on Angela. She went to clear the outside tables about ten minutes ago but hasn't reappeared. I can't imagine what's keeping her.'

'I can,' Flo murmured and the two of them smiled at each other.

Flo settled into the chair behind the till.

'It's great that Angela is helping with the shop, though. It takes the pressure off us a bit.'

'You can say that again.'

As Flo had suggested, Angela's help was making all the difference at All And Sundry.

She did two or three hours each day and the extra pair of hands meant that Penny and Flo weren't constantly trying to catch up with things. And the customers loved her cheerful nature.

She had even managed to persuade Brian and Eric to join the Cake Club, to Penny's great amusement. The two men now considered themselves to be cake experts and were happy to discuss at great length the moistness, crumble and flavour of each morning's offerings with anyone they managed to snare.

Penny made her way outside. It was just as she had expected. Angela had forgotten all about clearing the tables. Instead, she was doing a lively 'Macarena' with half a dozen others — mostly surfers, by the look of them — while Jordy played the music.

Some children were dancing, too, and many of the adults in the deckchairs were clapping along.

Penny smiled to herself. It was such a happy and relaxed atmosphere.

The dance came to an end, accompanied by whoops and cheers. One of the surfers grabbed Jordy's hat and carried it round the little crowd to collect contributions.

Angela spotted Penny and hurried over with a guilty look on her face.

'Sorry, Penny. I came out here to clear up the tables but I got a bit distracted.'

'Don't apologise. It was lovely to see the customers getting involved in the music. That's exactly what I want for All And Sundry, a sense of community about the place.'

She looked around with a grimace.

'It's just a pity that it looks so rough

out here. It would make such a difference if the area was properly landscaped.'

'That takes money, unfortunately,' Angela murmured.

Penny nodded.

'Money which we haven't got.'

The sprawling area beside the shop had been waste ground for as long as she could remember. Some people used it as an informal car park, others as a dumping ground for their garden waste and rubbish.

Over the years, weeds and bushes had sprung up all over the place.

Angela was gazing about with a thoughtful look on her face.

'It might be an expensive matter to landscape the whole area properly but what if you just wanted to clear it? Getting rid of the rubbish and undergrowth wouldn't be too hard, with the help of a few willing hands.'

'But where are the willing hands going to come from?'

Angela glanced over at the surfers who were playing air guitar round Jordy as he began to sing 'Summer Breeze'.

'As it happens, I do know a few strong young men who might be able to help. They would be a start.'

Help is at Hand

Penny looked round in amazement.

'It's fantastic! I can't believe this many people have turned up.'

Angela shrugged.

'The word just spread.'

It was Sunday morning and around 30 helpers had gathered at the waste ground outside All And Sundry. Apart from some of Angela and Jordy's surfing friends there were regular customers, people from neighbouring shops and friends of Bill and Maisie's.

Even Len Ryan, the local councillor, had come along to lend a hand. Flo's husband, Si, had set up his barbecue and sausages and burgers were already sizzling away.

'I had no idea we would get this much help,' Penny murmured, blinking away the tears welling up in her eyes.

'There's a lot of goodwill around for your mum and dad,' Brian said, pulling on his gardening gloves. 'Now, what do you want Eric and me to do?'

Penny climbed on to an old wooden box and clapped her hands to get everyone's attention.

'I can't thank you all enough for coming along this morning. Mum and Dad will be so proud when I tell them about this.'

'How's your dad doing?' someone shouted.

'He's fine. I spoke to him last night and he sounded full of beans. All I want is to ensure that All And Sundry is in good shape for when he and Mum decide that they're ready to come back and take over again.'

There was a sustained round of applause.

'Anyway, the plan this morning is to clear this bit of ground so that we can use it as an outdoor seating area. I want all the rubbish, rubble, shrubs and weeds put in that skip over there, which has been kindly loaned to us by our friends at Jamieson the Builders.'

She waved her arm.

'Once the ground is cleared, we'll cover it with bark mulch provided by the great folk at the Greenfingers Garden Centre. You'll have noticed that Si is already hard at work on the barbecue so once the bark is down then it will just be a case of helping him get rid of all the food he has produced. And there will be some beers and other refreshments available to help wash it down.'

There were a few whoops and cheers and then everyone scattered and got to work.

It was amazing how quickly things progressed. The skip was soon filling up with rubbish.

The atmosphere was cheerful and jokey and at one point the surfers even had everyone singing 'Whistle While You Work'.

Penny noticed Howard France standing on the pavement outside LoPrice watching what was going on. The supermarket was open seven days a week so there was nothing unusual

107

about him being there.

But from the look on his face, it didn't seem likely that he was planning to offer his help. So she was surprised when he started heading towards her.

'Hello, Mr France, how are you today?' she asked with a smile, determined not to let him spoil her afternoon.

He looked at her coldly for a moment.

'You do realise that there's a local by-law against building work being carried out on a Sunday.'

Penny looked at him uncertainly.

'A by-law?'

'This is a tourist town. The council doesn't want holidaymakers having their weekends spoilt by noise and dust. If you want to do building work on a Sunday then you have to make a proper application.

'I presume you've done that.' He looked around with a sarcastic expression. 'I don't see the notice of permission which is supposed to be publicly displayed.'

The sense of pleasure inside Penny

had drained away.

She felt suddenly foolish. She should have realised that it wasn't just a matter of gathering people together and getting on with the work.

Life was rarely that simple.

Then Len Ryan, the local councillor, appeared at her side.

'You know better than that, Howard,' he said calmly. 'The by-law you're referring to only applies to work being done by professional builders. Nobody is being paid here, we're all volunteers.'

'Are you sure it doesn't apply?' Penny asked in concern.

He nodded.

'I should know, I'm on the planning committee. Anyway, we're clearing up an eyesore in the middle of town. The council will be delighted about that.'

She turned to Howard France with a sense of relief, tinged with a feeling of triumph.

But he had already turned away and was striding off up the road back to LoPrice.

Len Ryan put a hand gently on her arm.

'Relax, Penny, you have nothing to worry about.'

Penny pushed all thoughts of Howard France to the back of her mind and looked around. Amazingly, the work was pretty much finished, thanks to the number of volunteers who had put in an appearance today.

What had been waste ground was now a pleasant area where people could sit around and enjoy the view.

And it was going to be for everyone, Penny decided, not just for All And Sundry customers.

The community had made it, so the community should be able to enjoy it.

Jordy's guitar was starting up, there was a crowd gathering round the barbecue and she could hear a clink of beer bottles from somewhere.

'Enough standing around, Penny,' she murmured to herself. 'You have work to do.'

She had a lot of thank-yous to say.

He is So Infuriating

Penny leaned against the railings of the promenade. She had started going to All And Sundry early each morning to sort out all the admin tasks.

The quietness allowed her to concentrate. Once the shop opened, she never seemed to have a moment to herself.

She gazed at the glorious view developing in front of her. The sun was about to appear over the hills at the far side of the bay and the sky was becoming a blaze of colour.

An old gent with a scraggy dog on a lead stopped beside her.

'Beautiful, isn't it?'

'You can say that again.'

They stood for a moment as the dog investigated a fish and chip wrapper on the ground. The clouds glowed yellow and red and fingers of pink began stretching across the sky in a sight that left Penny breathless.

Her companion shook his head.

'Seventy-three years I've lived in this place and it still manages to surprise me.'

'It's stunning.'

He gazed at her thoughtfully.

'Aren't you Bill and Maisie's daughter from All And Sundry?'

'That's right. I'm Penny.'

'I thought I recognised you. How is Bill?'

Penny smiled.

'Not bad at all. He and Mum are in the Lake District staying with my Auntie May. They said last night that they had started going on daily walks. I'm not surprised; it's such a beautiful place.'

'That's good to hear. Next time you speak, say that Frankie Weller was asking after them.'

'I will, Frankie. Thank you.'

Rather reluctantly, Penny turned away from the sunrise and carried on along the promenade.

She had spoken to her mum and dad the previous evening and her dad had sounded so relaxed. That day he had got chatting to a local fisherman who had suggested that Bill join him on his next trip. He had been really excited about it and had barely mentioned All And Sundry at all.

He was clearly settling well into life in the Lake District.

Penny turned the corner into Beach Road and then slowed with a frown. Graham Fraser was standing by All And Sundry gazing at the outside area.

Her eyes narrowed as she remembered the first time they had met. He had been wandering about the waste ground then as if he owned the place.

He looked round at the sound of her footsteps. To her surprise, a smile lit up his face.

'Hi, there, Penny.'

'Morning,' she said with little warmth in her voice.

'Did you see the sunrise? Wasn't it amazing?'

Penny glanced back. The sun had risen over the hills and the swirling colours in the sky were quickly disappearing.

'It was beautiful,' she admitted reluctantly.

'And now it's just another gorgeous day at the seaside.'

Despite herself, Penny felt herself responding to his smile. She remembered that first time they had met and how there had been things about him then that she had liked.

He did have a very natural way about him sometimes. And when he smiled his face seemed to light up.

He nodded to the area outside the shop.

'I was just admiring what you'd done with the waste ground here. It's not as if you've made massive changes, just cleared it and put down some bark chippings. But the whole place has been transformed.'

Penny was touched by the admiration in his voice. He was obviously impressed.

'I'm pleased with the way it's worked out.

People like sitting here and enjoying the view.'

'And you have live music playing here regularly as well.'

Penny nodded.

'That's Jordy. He tends to drop by in the afternoons and play for a while. The customers like it.'

Graham looked rueful.

'We have background music playing for our shoppers but it's not the same. I noticed yesterday afternoon that some of your customers were singing along with the music. It looked like a really good atmosphere.'

Penny found herself wondering if she had been mistaken about him. He was being perfectly friendly.

He looked at her for a moment.

'I know it's none of my business but something struck me while I was standing here.'

'Oh?' Penny said warily.

'Have you thought of putting a vending machine here outside the shop? Just selling snacks and soft drinks.'

Penny frowned.

'That hadn't occurred to me.'

'It would be a great position. There are plenty of passers-by in this street. And, of course, a vending machine would be working for you twenty-four hours a day.'

The more Penny thought about the idea, the more she liked it.

'Some companies are prepared to provide them at no cost — they simply take a slice of the profits. That way, you don't have to lay out lots of money up front.'

'That really could work,' Penny murmured. 'Thank you, Graham. That's a good suggestion.'

He smiled.

'No problem. We local businesses have to stick together.'

He took a card from his pocket and scribbled something on it.

'I've had some dealings with this firm in the past. They supply vending machines and I've found them quite reliable.'

Penny gazed at the card for a moment. It wasn't the company she was thinking of, it was Graham.

'Anyway, I'll leave you to get on with

your work. Have a good day.'

With a wave, he headed off to LoPrice.

'Bye, Graham — and thank you.'

Penny gazed after him, a thoughtful look on her face. Maybe she had been wrong about him.

She let herself into the shop. All thoughts of Graham were quickly driven from her mind as she got to grips with her To-Do list.

There were accounts to tally, Flo's wages to sort out, ordering to do.

But she also wanted to have a good think about the range of items they stocked. All And Sundry had always sold basic groceries but Penny wondered if the space they took up on the shelves could be used a bit more creatively.

For instance, the bread they sold was available in countless other shops in the area, including LoPrice, so it was unlikely to draw many customers into All And Sundry.

But what if they sold some specialist breads instead?

She had noticed in the local paper

an article about a small bakery which had recently opened up in the next town. The breads they were producing sounded quite unusual but also sounded delicious.

She wondered if it might be an idea to try selling some of their products.

Then there was the outside area. It desperately needed more reliable furnishings than old deckchairs and cardboard boxes for tables.

There was little or no money available in All And Sundry's kitty to buy anything, but Penny had been thinking about the furniture warehouse at the edge of town.

Might they be willing to supply furniture under some sort of arrangement? For instance, if they were able to advertise on the wall at the side of the shop?

She picked up the card Graham had given her. She recalled his suggestion of a vending machine. That was a real possibility.

As Penny worked away on her various admin tasks, her mind churned with ideas for the future.

* * *

'What's up with the lorries?' Angela asked that afternoon as she dropped two cups into the soapy water.

She had just done a round of the outside tables. For once, hardly anyone was sitting there.

Penny was gazing at the laptop behind the counter. She had been checking the All And Sundry Twitter feed. The day before, at Jordy's prompting, she had asked for suggestions for songs that he could play to the customers. All kinds of ideas were coming in, some sensible, some completely mad.

'What lorries?' she said absent-mindedly.

'There's one parked there on the road just outside the shop.'

Penny glanced up. It was a refrigerated lorry, the sort that delivered chilled readymeals and the like to supermarkets.

'That's OK, isn't it? Vehicles are allowed to park there.'

'Yes, but it's had its engine running for the past ten minutes. It stinks out there.'

Penny frowned. That might be why there was hardly anyone sitting at the tables.

'There was one there earlier, too,' Angela went on. 'A fruit and veg lorry.'

Penny's eyes suddenly narrowed.

'Hang on a minute. I noticed a lorry parked there this morning with its engine running. I thought at the time it was a bit odd.'

'They aren't delivering to us. They must be LoPrice lorries.'

Penny's face darkened with suspicion.

'Something is going on here,' she muttered. She moved from behind the counter and strode outside.

The driver of the lorry was sitting in his seat munching on a sandwich and gazing at a tabloid newspaper.

Penny rapped on his window. He turned and looked at her but made no other response.

Penny indicated that he should wind his window down. He gave an exaggerated sigh. With deliberate care, he put down his sandwich and then his newspaper, folding it carefully first.

He slowly wound down the window.

'Yeah?'

Penny tried not to sound too aggressive; there was no point in starting off on the wrong foot.

'Hi, I run this shop. I'm a bit concerned about the way you're parked here.'

He leaned out of the window and looked up and down the road.

'It's legal, isn't it? There are no yellow lines.'

'Yes, but you're running your engine.'

His gave a twist of his mouth.

'My battery's low. It needs charging up.'

'But our shop is being filled with your exhaust fumes. No-one wants to have coffee and cake with that smell in the air.'

He shrugged.

'Not my problem.'

'There's more space to park just up the road. You could move there and then you wouldn't be bothering anyone.'

He looked at the space for a few moments and turned back to her.

'I could. But I'm not going to.'

He began to wind up the window. Penny's suspicions were becoming stronger by the moment.

'Have you been instructed to do this?'

'Don't know what you're talking about,' he retorted as the window closed.

Turning his back on her inside the cab, he picked up the paper and began reading it again with exaggerated concentration.

Penny went slowly back into the shop.

'That's not a happy look,' Angela murmured.

'We're being messed around,' Penny retorted, 'and I don't like it one little bit.'

Though she wasn't sure what she could do about it.

It was about five minutes later, as she was dealing with a customer, when she heard the lorry's engine revving. Its brakes were released with a squeal and it slowly set off up the road.

Once Penny had finished with the customer, she made her way outside. The lorry had moved just up the road to LoPrice.

With a sour feeling in her stomach, she saw Graham directing it into the delivery area next to the supermarket's car park.

'I might have guessed,' she muttered to herself.

She stepped back into the shop.

'Flo, Angela, I'm just going to deal with something. I'll be back in a few minutes.'

The short walk to LoPrice was long enough for a bubbling rage to build up inside her. Graham had seemed so friendly that morning with his praise about the outdoor area and his suggestion about the vending machine. But she should have known that it was too good to be true.

He noticed her as she strode towards him and a welcoming smile brightened up his face.

'Hi, Penny, are you all right?' His smile faltered as he saw her expression.

'I want a word with you.'

He looked at her uncertainly.

'Yes, of course.'

He turned to the driver who was climbing out of the lorry.

'You'll find the warehouse supervisor just through that door. He'll get a couple of helpers to sort out the unloading.'

He turned back to Penny.

'How can I help you?'

Penny pointed at the lorry.

'For the past fifteen minutes, that lorry has been parked on the pavement outside All And Sundry with its engine running.'

He frowned as if he wasn't quite sure what point she was making.

'That happens from time to time. We only have space for one delivery lorry. If a second turns up then it has to wait its turn.'

'So you've had another delivery lorry being unloaded all this time, have you?'

He looked slightly uncomfortable.

'As it happens, the last one left about half an hour ago, so I'm not quite sure …'

'And when your lorries are waiting, do they have to park outside All And Sundry?' Penny demanded. 'And do they have to leave their engines running so our customers have to put up with toxic fumes?'

'I'm not sure what you're trying to suggest.'

'I'm not *trying* to suggest anything,' Penny retorted, feeling her temper begin to slip out of control. 'I am saying that LoPrice delivery lorries have been deliberately trying to drive away our customers today.'

Graham burst out laughing.

'Now I think you're being a bit fanciful.'

'Don't you dare laugh at me!'

'What's going on here?'

It was Howard France, the LoPrice boss. He strode towards them, glaring at Graham.

'Is there a problem?'

'Yes, there is,' Penny snapped before Graham could reply. 'You're messing around with our business and I'm not going to put up with it.'

He snorted in derision.

'What nonsense. Why on earth would a store like LoPrice be concerned about a tiny shop such as yours?'

The open contempt in his voice only infuriated Penny further.

'You want us to go out of business, don't you?' she snapped. 'Because then you can buy up our land and expand your tawdry little empire.'

His eyes flared.

'Rubbish, total rubbish.' He turned and strode away. 'Deal with this, Fraser, and be quick about it,' he called over his shoulder.

Graham looked at Penny, his hands held out in a placatory manner.

'I think you were mistaken about the lorry. It may have been parked outside All And Sundry but that had nothing to do with your business. It was just a coincidence that … '

'I'm not wrong and it's not a coincidence.' She lifted a finger and pointed it at him. 'You leave us alone at All And Sundry or I'm warning you, there will be trouble.'

She turned away before he had a chance to reply.

'Are you all right?' Angela asked as she stomped into the shop.

Penny grabbed a dishtowel and hurled it against the wall.

'That man — he is so infuriating!'

A Cloud of Gloom

'I can't decide whether to do ginger snaps for the children's biscuits tomorrow or try lemon digestives for a change. What do you reckon, Miss Penny?'

'For goodness sake, Flo, just choose the one you think best. Do I have to decide everything around here?'

Penny instantly regretted her words. She looked at Flo's shocked face and stretched out a hand.

'Oh Flo, I'm so sorry. I don't know what's got into me this morning. I was bad-tempered with Angela at breakfast and now I'm being rude to you.'

The fact was that she hadn't slept very well the night before. She had kept mentally replaying the meeting she'd had with Graham.

She found him so annoying. She told herself that she should just forget about him — it would be better all round if he was simply out of her life altogether. Yet she couldn't seem to dismiss him from her mind and that was partly because she wasn't happy with her own behaviour.

The way things had ended between them the day before hadn't been satisfactory.

'This is ridiculous,' she muttered to herself, lying irritable and awake in bed.

She looked at her watch. It was five-thirty in the morning. Wearily, she got up and wrapped the duvet round herself. It was obvious that she wasn't going to get back to sleep.

She went over to the window and pulled back the curtain. Weale Bay stretched out in front of her. The tide was coming in and silver slivers from the moon's reflection danced over the water looking like something out of a fairytale. But for once the glorious view wasn't enough to raise her spirits.

So she got up with a headache, banged around the kitchen for a while and then snapped at Angela when she came to find out if something was up.

It hadn't been a great start to the day.

She placed a hand now gently on Flo's arm.

'I really am sorry.'

Flo's look of concern was replaced by a cheery smile.

'That's all right, Miss Penny — you have a lot on your mind. Now, will you be fine to open up if I get on with the baking?'

'Of course I will. And let's hope we have a great day at All And Sundry.'

Penny began to set up the tables and chairs on the pavement. She shivered slightly. The weather seemed to be changing. The cloud was thickening up and there was a chill in the air.

She could see a few people scattered about the beach but most of them were wrapped up warmly.

'Morning.' A passer-by with a newspaper under his arm nodded.

'Morning,' Penny replied.

'Not so warm today. There's a storm on its way, they say.'

'I saw that on the TV last night.'

The forecaster had suggested that the weather was going to get steadily worse over the next couple of days. There was likely to be a lot of rain and in some areas there was the possibility of flooding.

Penny brought out the deckchairs and leaned them against the wall so that people could help themselves.

She looked around with a frown. Having an outside area at All And Sundry was all very well but it depended on good weather.

There was no protection for customers from the rain.

'Or from the sun, either,' she muttered to herself. Not everyone was a sun-lover.

Some people preferred sitting in the shade on sunny days.

She wondered about the possibility of having an awning fitted to the side of the shop — or perhaps a gazebo built.

Ideas began to stir in her head. Maybe there could be a serving hatch fitted into the wall so that it was simpler to collect and deliver orders for the customers outside.

Could they have one of those trampolines set into the ground for children to bounce on, wooden play equipment, crazy golf?

She smiled to herself as she headed back into the shop. If her mum and dad won the lottery one day, then perhaps there would be enough money to try out all her ideas for All And Sundry — but probably not before.

Then she stopped. Graham was outside LoPrice. He was filling up the container of barbecue packs and firewood by the entrance.

Her stomach gave a sour twist. She felt a sudden urge to hurry over to him and ... and what? She wasn't sure. Not to apologise, she had nothing to apologise for.

Perhaps just to make things right between them. There had been times when they had seemed to get on well together. She had liked that. She had felt that he was someone whose company she would enjoy.

She watched him, hoping that he

would turn and spot her. They could smile at each other and wave.

She could ask him if he wanted to meet up some time, she suddenly thought.

A spurt of excitement went though her. It wouldn't be a proper date — just getting together for coffee maybe, or for a drink after work. It would be nice to get to know him better.

But even as she was thinking about how she might word the suggestion, he placed the last bag of firewood in the container and headed back into LoPrice with the empty trolley. He hadn't even seen her.

Penny gazed at the empty space where he had been standing and felt a sense of loss.

It was as if an opportunity had been there but now it was gone.

'Morning, Penny, how are you today?'

She looked round and forced a smile on to her face.

'Morning, Brian. Morning, Eric. In you come and I'll get your cups of tea.'

'I wouldn't mind another piece of the

millionaire's shortbread I had yesterday,'
Brian said. 'Very tasty, that was.'
'I'll see if there's some left.'
They followed her into the shop.
'Are you all right, Penny?' Eric asked
with a searching look. 'You seem a bit …
well, not your usual sparky self.'
Penny smiled weakly.
'I'm fine, thanks, Brian. I'll see to
those teas.'
But as she got to work behind the
counter, she didn't feel particularly fine.
On any other day, she would have
been in good spirits. The chill in the air
meant that lazing on the beach wasn't
proving such an attraction. Lots of holidaymakers were wandering around the
local shops and entertainments instead.
A warming cup of tea or coffee was
just what they were looking for and All
And Sundry was soon drawing in the
customers.
But she was finding it difficult to throw
off the cloud of gloom hanging round
her.
When Angela turned up after her

morning surf, Penny immediately took the opportunity to apologise.

'I'm sorry about this morning. I was so grumpy with you when I was having my breakfast!'

Angela just laughed.

'Forget it, babe. Everyone is entitled to be grumpy at that time in the morning.'

Penny couldn't help smiling. She doubted that anything was capable of spoiling Angela's good spirits. Since she and Jordy had got together, a glow of happiness had seemed to surround her wherever she went.

'Is Jordy not with you?'

Angela shook her head.

'He and a bunch of the other surfers have something on. I'm not sure what, they were discussing it when I left. I think they must be going somewhere because they were trying to work out how many cars they had between them.'

Angela looked around and clapped her hands together.

'Anyway, here I am ready for work.

What would you like me to get on with?'

With Flo in the back baking and Angela looking after the customers, Penny had time to have a quick check on the shop's emails and Twitter feed. #AllAndSundry was really starting to take off, particularly with customers taking selfies of themselves as the Star Wars figures and then posting the pictures online.

Word was definitely starting to get out about the shop.

Wow — we're going on holiday to Weale next week. We'll have to check out #AllAndSundry. Sounds cool! one tweet said.

Penny felt her feeling of gloom dissipating as she read the various messages. Social media was such a good way of advertising the shop, especially as it didn't cost anything apart from her time.

She came across a tweet praising All And Sundry to the skies. Penny didn't recognise the name. *@BellaFisher*. Then she saw the two photos — one of the family standing outside the shop with their poodle, the other of a biscuit with the name *Napoleon* on it.

The brilliant folk at #AllAndSundry wrote our dog's name on a biscuit today. Love it!!!

The post had been retweeted dozens of times with many people liking it.

Penny gazed at the post, her eyes narrowing thoughtfully.

Just then, Angela hurried over.

'Quick question — there's a family here wondering if they could get their dog's name written on one of our biscuits. That would be all right, wouldn't it?'

'There's a coincidence!' Penny laughed. 'Of course it's fine.'

She turned back to her phone and did a quick search for 'Dog biscuit recipes'. To her surprise, there were all kinds of suggestions.

She smiled to herself. Once Flo was on the case, All And Sundry could add personalised dog biscuits to the items it had to sell.

Another idea suddenly struck her.

'Eric,' she asked, 'do cats eat biscuits?'

She knew that he had a couple of cats at home.

'Eh?'

'What do you think of the idea of people buying personalised biscuits for their cats?'

Brian gazed at her with a mixture of alarm and concern.

'Maybe your dad's not the only one in the family who needs a break.'

Penny grinned. Maybe he was right. Perhaps that idea needed a bit more thinking through.

It was around mid-afternoon when Penny first got wind of the trouble at LoPrice. It had been a busy day and, as she served the two customers, her mind was on the grocery order which she needed to put in.

There was also the idea of installing a vending machine — she wanted to contact the company before the end of the day.

So she wasn't really paying attention to their conversation as she rang up their bill. But then she heard what they were saying.

'I don't know what's going on at LoPrice but it seems a bit chaotic,' one lady said.

Her companion nodded.

'When I went past, there were lots of people with cars trapped in the car park.

They couldn't get them out.'

'I saw a couple of lorries waiting in the road as well. They couldn't make their deliveries.'

She shook her head.

'I gave one driver a piece of my mind. He shouldn't have used that sort of language when there were children nearby.'

Penny looked at them in puzzlement.

'Did you say there was trouble at LoPrice?'

The woman nodded.

'In the car park. Some idiots have blocked the entrance so that no-one can get in or out. Things were in a right state when I went past.'

Quickly finishing the sale, Penny went outside to have a look. It was difficult to make out what was going on exactly. There were two lorries on the street, clearly waiting to get into the LoPrice delivery area, while in the car park itself there was a long line of cars waiting to get out.

But nothing was able to move because three rather tatty-looking cars were parked across the entrance, blocking it completely.

Penny could see Graham surrounded by people. He seemed to be trying to calm them down but even at that distance she could hear the raised voices. There was clearly a lot of anger around.

Howard France was striding about, shouting into a phone, his arms gesticulating wildly. He finished the call with a furious gesture.

He spotted Penny. He gazed at her for a moment and then pointed at her.

'That's who is responsible for this!'

He strode angrily down the pavement towards her, a few people following him.

'You're behind this, aren't you?' he shouted as he approached.

Graham, behind him, put a hand on his shoulder.

'Let's take it easy.'

Howard France pushed him roughly away.

'Get off me.' He turned back to Penny and waved a finger in her face. 'You are going to regret this.'

'I've no idea what you're talking about,' Penny said in bafflement. 'Regret what?'

'Don't act the innocent. It's obvious that you organised the blockade of our car park.'

'Me?'

'Well, you're not going to get away with it and that's a promise.'

Penny held out her arms.

'I don't know what you're talking about. Whatever is going on at LoPrice, it has nothing to do with us here at All And Sundry.'

He waved a hand at her and turned away, pressing his phone against his ear.

'You can tell the police that when they get here.'

As he strode off, Graham came over

to her side.

'I'm sorry about that. You'll have to forgive Mr France, he's really upset. It's been chaos at LoPrice for the past hour or so.'

'Maybe, but the problems you're having are nothing to do with me,' Penny retorted.

She wasn't sure why but she really wanted him to believe her.

After a moment, he just nodded as if he accepted what she had said.

He sighed.

'I'm sorry that there have been problems between our two businesses. It would be a lot better for both of us if we cooperated with each other.'

'That's exactly what I feel,' Penny replied eagerly.

She found herself looking at his eyes. They were a greeny colour with flecks of blue and there were wrinkles at the corners as if he was used to laughing.

She felt a smile drift on to her face. She liked the idea of the two of them laughing together.

'Fraser, hurry up,' came Howard France's angry shout. 'There's work needing done.'

With a last momentary glance, Graham turned away.

Storm on the Way

Penny splashed along the promenade, huddling as best she could under her dad's golf umbrella. Someone scurried past in the other direction and for once there was no exchange of greetings; the downpour made sure of that.

The early-morning forecast had been bleak. Heavy rain was expected all day with increasing winds and, over the next 24 hours, the weather was likely to get worse.

She and Angela had slipped into the habit of getting up about the same time each morning. They sat round the kitchen table for a while, having some breakfast and chatting about the day ahead.

Then Angela would head off to her surfing while Penny made her way to All And Sundry. But that morning, when Angela saw the state of the weather, she took her cup of coffee and headed straight back to bed.

'I'll see you later at the shop.' She smiled.

The wind caught the umbrella and, for a moment, Penny's face was soaked by pelting rain. Waves were surging in all directions and she could feel them crashing against the sea wall.

She gazed at the water running in a hurried stream along the edge of the road. If it was like this now, what would it be like when the weather got even worse?

'Fresh morning!' came a voice. Penny glanced up from under the umbrella to see a grizzled old man covered head-to-toe with yellow oilskins.

The grin on his face suggested that a little bit of rain didn't bother him in the slightest though, to Penny's amusement, his dog didn't seem to be sharing his enjoyment. It looked drenched and miserable.

'You can say that again,' she called over her shoulder as she hurried on.

She unlocked the door of the shop and a car drove past, sending a spray of water on to the pavement. She had to jump out of the way to avoid it.

She looked at the road uncertainly. She didn't much like the way the water was collecting there.

Penny let herself in and decided that there was no point in putting tables and chairs out. No-one would want to sit outside on a day like this.

Thoughts started mulling in her head. The shop was only really set up for good weather. There was no particular plan for when things got worse.

She checked the Twitter feed. There were a healthy number of messages.

More customers had posted selfies of themselves outside the shop, there were votes for favourite cakes from the day before, and someone had shared a picture of their dog with an All And Sundry biscuit balanced on its nose.

Penny's eyes narrowed as she suddenly had a thought. Her fingers got to work.

#RainyDayIdeas. How could All And Sundry make the most of a day like this? A free slice of cake for the 10 best suggestions.

She posted the message. She didn't suppose anything very useful would come of it but it was another way to get people thinking about the shop.

She began searching through a pile of papers to find the order list she had made up the day before. Just as she spotted it, a new message appeared on the Twitter feed.

Penny clicked on it.

#RainyDayIdeas – Fit a water slide to the roof of the shop!

She smiled. Another message appeared.

Set up a fish farm in the rain barrel outside. #RainyDayIdeas.

A few moments later came another.

Wet T-shirt competition for customers and staff. #RainyDayIdeas.

Penny burst out laughing as she imagined Flo's face if she suggested that.

'Goodness, what a morning,' Flo said when she arrived 40 minutes later.

'I have seen better.' Penny smiled.

Flo stamped her feet and shook the rain from her coat before coming into the shop.

'That was quite a to-do at LoPrice yesterday.'

Penny nodded.

'The boss was in a right state.'

Her mouth twisted for a moment as she remembered his accusations.

'I'm not sure what happened in the end.'

Flo sat down beside her eagerly.

'I was talking to my neighbour, Delia, last night. She was trapped in the car park for over an hour and she was steaming.'

'Did she know what it was all about?'

Flo shrugged.

'Apparently some local lads parked their cars in the car park entrance and just left them there. It was chaos. No-one knew what was going on and Howard France was furious.'

'That's putting it mildly,' Penny retorted.

'In the end, he contacted the police,' Flo said.

'And did they deal with it?'

Flo shook her head.

'Before the police got there, these three young chaps just appeared, got in the cars and drove off.'

'What, just like that?'

Flo nodded.

'Howard France tried to stop them leaving but they ignored him. Delia said he was in such a rage, threatening all sorts of things.'

'What happened when the police got there?'

Flo shrugged.

'Nothing much. They were given the registration numbers of the cars but they said that because the problem had been sorted they weren't going to take any further action.'

'That made Howard France even angrier. The police had to warn him to calm down, Delia said.'

Penny shook her head.

'Weird. But I suppose things did get resolved in the end.'

Flo looked at her watch and began putting on her apron.

'Anyway, I'd better get baking.'

'And I'd better open up.'

Penny had another quick glance at the Twitter feed. To her amazement, dozens of rainy day ideas had been added. Most were a bit bonkers and impractical but one caught her attention.

We're at Weale-On-Sea, it's pouring with rain and I've got 3 children. What are we going to do all day!?! #DesperateMum #RainyDayIdeas.

Penny's brain suddenly went into overdrive. There must be lots of families in that situation. She hurried through to the back of the shop.

'Flo, is Si at home?'

'He should be. Unless he's been contacted about a job.'

Her husband, Si, was a taxi driver.

'I've got a job for him — an urgent one.'

'Well, give him a call.'

Minutes later, Penny was heading with Si in his taxi to the local cash-and-carry, having left a notice on the door of All And Sundry saying that the shop might be slightly late in opening.

At the store, she began searching for anything on the shelves that might keep children occupied on a rainy day.

The taxi was soon packed with jigsaws, colouring books, construction sets, watercolours, paint-by-number sets, board games and puzzle books.

As Si drove her back to All And Sundry, she began pricing up the items, adding a straight 10% to whatever she had paid.

When they arrived at the shop, Brian and Eric were waiting huddled in the doorway.

'You two are just what I need,' Penny said. 'How would you like to earn a free cup of tea each?'

Brian looked at her suspiciously.

'And a slice of cake?'

'It's a deal.'

They helped her carry her purchases inside. Then, once the window area had been cleared, Penny asked if they would organise the items she had bought into some sort of display.

They took up the challenge eagerly

and, to Penny's amusement, a disagree-
ment quickly developed between them.
Brian wanted everything looking neat
and organised while Eric thought the
items should be arranged more infor-
mally.

Neither was prepared to give way and
the argument raged.

Meanwhile, Penny was hard at work
on a poster. On a large sheet of paper, she
wrote *#RainyDayIdeas* in giant letters.
Round the edges she doodled pictures
of children playing.

She stuck the poster up in the window.

'Right, gents, are you ready for that
cup of tea?'

'But the display is a mess,' Brian said,
gazing at it in disapproval.

He was right — some things were in
tidy piles while others were scattered
about in a completely haphazard way.

Penny just shrugged.

'Does that matter? It's going to end
up in a mess anyway, when customers
start searching through the items. The
important thing is that there are plenty

of rainy day activities for people to choose from.'

It was a quiet morning in the shop with the rain outside not easing up at all.

However, the window display was a definite success. Lots of holidaymakers were wandering miserably round the streets trying to find some way to occupy themselves and the #RainyDayIdeas sign grabbed their attention.

There was usually someone gazing at the items through the window or inside the shop looking through them.

Angela turned up around mid-morning.

'I like that,' she said, nodding towards the window.

Penny smiled.

'It was a spur-of-the-moment idea but it's doing not too badly. People need an alternative when they can't spend the day on the beach, especially families with young children. I don't suppose there's much surfing going on today, either?'

'I've just been down at the Surfing Shack,' Angela said.

She looked at Penny uncertainly.

'Actually, there's something I wanted to talk to you about. You know the problems at LoPrice yesterday?'

Penny nodded.

'I was speaking to Flo about it earlier. She said it was three young blokes.'

Angela nodded.

'Three young surfers.'

Penny looked at her sharply.

'What?'

'Deano, Bri and Zack. They were talking about it this morning. They thought it was a big joke.'

'A joke?'

'Some of the guys had heard about the lorries parking outside All And Sundry with their engines running. They decided to give the LoPrice boss a taste of his own medicine.'

'But he thinks that I was responsible!' Penny cried. 'Arguments between us and LoPrice are the last thing we need at the moment.'

'That's what I said,' Angela replied. 'If they thought they were doing All And Sundry a favour then they were making a big mistake.'

'Maybe I should speak to the three of them.' Penny sighed.

Angela thought for a moment.

'I'll be seeing them later. I can make sure they get the message loud and clear.'

'OK.'

Penny chewed her lip for a moment.

'Could you keep an eye on the shop for a bit, Angela? I'm going next door to sort all this out. The arguments between our two businesses have gone on far too long.'

'No problem.'

Penny hurried up the road to LoPrice. She wasn't very sure what she was going to say.

It wasn't her job to inform on the people responsible for the troubles the day before.

On the other hand, she wanted to make it clear that it had been nothing to do with her.

She spotted Graham by the drinks display, checking something off on a clipboard. She went over to him.

'Hi, there.'

When he turned, his face lit up.

'Penny, hi. How are you?' He was obviously pleased to see her.

She hesitated, not certain how to begin.

'I wanted a quick word.'

'Yes, of course.'

'It's about the problems yesterday in the car park.'

He grimaced and shook his head.

'Penny, I never thought that you were responsible. I'm sure that Mr France didn't really either. It was just a very stressful situation and ... well, accusations were made that possibly shouldn't have been.'

'That's the thing,' Penny went on. 'I know who was responsible.'

Graham's eyes widened and she hurried on.

'I knew nothing about it at the time. But I've just learned that it was some young lads who had heard about the business with the lorries parked outside All And Sundry with their engines running. They thought that they would arrange some payback.'

'I knew it!'

Penny whirled round. Howard France was standing in the doorway beside the drinks display. He strode forward, his eyes blazing with triumph.

'I knew that you were involved somehow. Well, you're going to be hearing from our lawyers about this.'

'Your lawyers?'

He waved his arms in the air, his voice growing louder.

'Have you any idea how much money that nonsense cost LoPrice yesterday? Our takings in the afternoon were way down. And you were responsible.'

'I really don't think ...' Graham began.

'We're both witnesses. She admitted in our hearing that the people responsible for the chaos yesterday were doing it because of All And Sundry.'

Graham frowned.

'I wouldn't put it quite like that.'

'You heard what I heard — and the court is going to be hearing it, too.' He waved a finger in Penny's face. 'You are going to pay dearly for what you did.'

Without waiting for a reply, he turned and hurried off.

'I'm sorry,' Graham said quietly. 'I don't suppose that was what you were hoping for when you came here.'

Penny didn't know what to say. She just lifted a hand and turned away. She walked down the road to All And Sundry, heedless of the rain falling on her.

Her whole reason for looking after the shop over the summer had been to take the stress off her mum and dad. But if lawyers' letters were going to start arriving with threats of court action, that would just make their stress a hundred times worse.

She gazed into the All And Sundry window. Almost all the items she had bought at the cash-and-carry that morning were gone. The only things left were a jigsaw, a watercolour set and a couple

158

of puzzle books.

She should have been delighted at the success of the idea. But as rain dribbled down the back of her shirt, all she felt was a grey cloud of gloom.

Flood Alert

'Storm Celia is still in its early stages but heavy overnight rain has already resulted in flooding in some areas. The situation is expected to grow worse over the course of the day, particularly on the South coast.'

'That's us.' Penny sighed to herself.

'And with strong winds and torrential rain expected, you are advised only to travel if absolutely necessary.' The TV presenter gazed from the screen with a sympathetic smile. 'Good luck out there.'

Her colleague nodded.

'Good luck indeed. It sounds like a day for wrapping yourself in the duvet with a mug of hot chocolate and a wide selection of snacks and staying in bed.'

Penny snorted.

'If only.'

'Now, there's a plan. And, of course, we'll be here to keep you company.'

'Oh, no, you won't.'

Penny switched off the TV and put her breakfast dishes in the sink.

She gazed out of the kitchen window. Rain was pelting against the glass and the branches of the trees across the road were swaying wildly in the wind.

She chewed her lower lip. It wasn't far to All And Sundry but, if she wasn't careful, she was going to end up soaked.

She glanced at her phone. There was just the message Angela had sent the previous evening to say that she was spending the night at Jordy's and would see Penny in the shop around mid-morning.

A smile flicked across her face.

Don't worry too much about the shop, she texted back . *We're not going to be very busy today. You and Jordy should spend the day huddling together for warmth.*

She looked around. The question now was how to get herself to the shop without becoming drenched in the process . . .

'Looking good.' Graham laughed later as he hurried past her under a large umbrella.

Penny grinned.

'It's the latest summer fashion.'

'Good luck today!' he called out.

'You, too.'

Her wet hands fumbled with the keys.

'Come on, come on,' she muttered.

But soon she was in the shop and the door was closed behind her. She stood for a moment. It was such a relief to be out of the pounding rain.

She looked down at herself. She had found some of her dad's wet-weather gear in the utility room. There were the waterproof dungarees that he sometimes used for fishing, a yellow oilskin coat, a great floppy hat and wellies that were a number of sizes too big.

She smiled as she thought of the amused expression on Graham's face. She stamped her feet and shook her arms.

At least her unusual outfit meant that she had got to All And Sundry with her clothes still dry and only a few wet strands of hair plastered across her face.

She went through to the back of the

shop, removed her outer layers and hung them up. She found herself thinking of the interaction between herself and Graham. It had been light-hearted and friendly for a change, as if the awkward-ness between them had gone.

She was pleased about that.

'Goodness, this is very cheerful, Miss Penny,' Flo said as she arrived later.

The sound of summer music filled the shop and balloons were hanging from the ceiling, swinging gently from side to side.

'I decided that everyone would need cheering up when they came into All And Sundry today.' Penny smiled.

Then she looked at Flo in puzzlement.

'How come you're not wet? It's pour-ing down outside and it's getting heavier.'

Flo grinned.

'That's one of the advantages of being married to a taxi driver. Si gave me a lift.'

Her eye was caught by a new poster which had appeared in the window. It bore large fluorescent letters.

Sand Art Competition today. Amazing

Prizes. Free Flapjack With Every Entry.

'What's that all about, then?'

Penny nodded to a corner of the shop.

She had set up a table with a large tray of sand. Beside it was a laptop, switched on and waiting.

'It's just an idea.'

Flo laughed.

'You're good at those.'

'We're bound to be a bit short on customers today with the weather the way it is. So I thought that a sand art competition might drag a few more in off the street.'

Flo was looking at the sand in puzzlement.

'What do people have to do?'

'Just make a picture in the sand.' Penny started drawing a large round face with her finger. She added glasses, sticking up hair, earrings and a bushy beard. 'I'll take a digital photo of each entry and put it on the laptop. I've set it up to show the pictures for a few seconds each on a continuous loop. It's just a bit of fun, really.'

'And what are the amazing prizes?'

Penny grinned.

'I haven't actually thought about that yet. I'm sure I'll come up with something.'

Flo shook her head in admiration.

'You and your ideas, Miss Penny.'

Penny shrugged.

'Anything to attract more customers.'

She brought out her phone and took a photo of her drawing. Then she rubbed the sand flat again.

'Anyway, we need a few pictures on the laptop to encourage people so come on, Flo, that's your first job of the day. Draw something in the sand.'

Penny had expected Flo to protest and say that she was no good at drawing. Instead, she was looking at the sand thoughtfully.

'OK.'

Penny went to open up the shop. The rain was teeming down outside. A car went slowly by, the driver clearly being careful not to splash people on the pavements.

Penny gazed at the streams of water pouring down the road towards the promenade. It looked as if the drains were already filled to overflowing.

A worried frown settled over her face. If the water got much higher, it could become a problem.

'What do you think?' Flo asked as Penny returned.

Penny blinked.

'That's amazing, Flo.' It was a simple beach scene but beautifully drawn.

Flo's cheeks tinged with pleasure.

'I always enjoyed doing art at school.'

'Why have I been doing our posters all this time, when we have someone with real talent working here in the shop?'

'I wouldn't say that.'

'Well, I would.' Penny took a photo of the drawing and cleared the sand. 'OK, before you do anything else, I want three more sand pictures to put on the laptop.'

She grinned.

'You never know, Flo, you could be in line for one of our amazing prizes – whatever they are.'

* * *

As Penny had expected, things were slow in All And Sundry. Bill and Eric were the first customers, though that was no surprise.

Some rather miserable holidaymakers came in, trying to find somewhere to shelter out of the rain. Penny had put out a few extra chairs and they were soon put to good use.

The weather outside was getting worse and, around mid-morning, Angela and Jordy burst into the shop hand-in-hand. Their laughter as they stood dripping at the entrance seemed to light up the whole place.

'It's 'Agadoo'!' Angela cried, as a new song started to play over the speakers.

She grabbed Jordy and the two of them began doing the actions.

'A – ga – do – do – do, push pineapple shake the tree … '

Two children joined in, followed by their parents. Jordy pulled Eric to his feet and Angela even overcame Bill's reluctance.

Before long, virtually everyone in All And Sundry was taking part in the song.

A rather confused-looking shopper came in at one point, gazed around in bafflement and then found himself pulled into the melee by Angela before he knew what was happening. There were cheers and whoops all round when the song eventually finished.

Somehow, Angela and Jordy's good spirits infected everyone. The two of them had a go at the sand art competition and then insisted that other customers do so as well.

On such a miserable day, their cheerfulness came as a welcome relief.

Penny smiled to herself as Angela did a mock commentary of the sand art pictures coming up on the laptop with Jordy leading the cheers for each of them.

Penny smiled to herself. No-one was buying very much and All And Sundry was unlikely to make much of a profit over the course of the day. But the little shop was filled with a great atmosphere.

'Let's Twist Again' started playing.

'Come on, Penny,' Angela cried, grabbing her and pulling her into the middle of the floor.

Penny didn't try to resist. Angela in that sort of mood was unstoppable.

The rain didn't let up throughout the day. By mid-afternoon, the streets were empty of passers-by.

At one point, Bill phoned her.

'I was listening to the weather forecast for the Weale area. It doesn't sound great.'

Penny laughed.

'That's the understatement of the year, Dad. It's been terrible! We're not going to make our fortunes today. We haven't had a customer for the last half hour.'

'In that case, I would shut up shop and go home. There's no point hanging around for no reason.'

Penny gazed at her phone in disbelief.

'Shut the shop? What's got into you, Dad?'

He laughed.

'It must be the relaxing influence of

the Lake District.'

'It's a nice idea but I think I should hang around and keep an eye on things,' Penny said. 'There's a lot of water on the street outside.'

'That shouldn't be a problem. It'll all flow down to the promenade and into the sea.'

'I hope you're right but I'll stick around for a bit, anyway.'

As the call ended, Angela came over to the counter.

'Would it be OK if Jordy and I left now?'

'Of course. It's not like we're over-whelmed here.' Then she saw the worried look on Angela's face. 'Why, is something wrong?'

She nodded.

'Jordy just had a text from someone at the Surfing Shack. The water is starting to gather round the entrance there — they're worried that it might get in. We want to see if we can help.'

'Of course, off you go. I hope everything is all right.'

As Jordy and Angela hurried off, Penny gazed outside. The rain wasn't letting up at all. She turned to Flo.

'Flo, you might as well go home, too.'

'Are you sure, Miss Penny?'

'Get Si to come and pick you up.'

Flo nodded and smiled.

As Penny closed the door behind Flo, she gazed at the water streaming down the road. It was close to reaching the pavement.

If that happened, it wouldn't be long before it was at All And Sundry's doorway.

She didn't care what her dad had said, she was going nowhere.

She locked up the shop, got a chair and parked herself near the doorway so that she could keep an eye on things. With a cup of coffee in one hand and a book in the other, she was soon lost in a romantic mystery.

It was about half an hour later when a knock at the door dragged her mind away from the heroine's predicament.

It was Graham.

'Come in,' she said, quickly getting to her feet.

He shook the rain off his coat as she closed the door behind him.

'I saw the light on in the shop. I just wondered how things were here.'

'I'm a bit worried about the amount of water outside.'

He nodded.

'We've been quite concerned at LoPrice too. We put some sandbags round the front and back entrances. Mr France is looking after things now. I've finished for the day.'

'We shut up shop a while back. But I thought I'd stay on for a while.'

He hesitated.

'Would you like me to stay for a bit?'

Penny's eyes widened.

'I couldn't ask you to do that.'

'Not a problem. I'd only be going back to my flat to heat up a ready meal.' He looked at her. 'To be honest, I'd like the chance.

I've been feeling for ages that the two of us didn't get off on the right foot.'

172

Penny nodded slowly.

'I've been feeling exactly the same myself.' She smiled. 'Would you like a coffee?'

'That would be great.'

'And maybe a slice of Flo's banana cake?'

He grinned.

'I have heard rumours about Flo's baking.'

'They're not exaggerated. She's a wonder in the kitchen.'

Penny started getting the cups ready but then Graham held out a hand.

'Hang on, what's that?'

'What's what?'

'That noise.'

They listened for a moment. Penny gasped.

'Oh, my goodness, is that running water?'

Water, Water Everywhere

Penny raced to the back of the shop. Her immediate thought was that there might be a burst pipe. But the kitchen was fine and she realised that the noise was coming from the storeroom.

She hurriedly pressed the light switch by the doorway and then screamed in shock as there was a flash from the ceiling and an explosion of sparks. Darkness fell over the room.

'Be careful!' Graham cried, grabbing her by the shoulder. 'Water must have got into the electrics. Do you have a torch?'

Penny tried to think but her mind seemed to have seized up. She shook her head.

'I'm not sure … I don't think so.'

'Don't worry, I've got one in my car. I'll be back in a moment. Don't do anything,' he called out as he hurried off.

Penny peered into the darkness of

the storeroom. She could make out the blurred shapes of items piled against the wall. The noise of the water was coming from somewhere at the back.

There was a step leading down into the storeroom. She put her hand carefully against the wall to steady herself and took a pace forward. She hurriedly moved back again. It was wet.

With a sickening feeling, she realised that the whole storeroom floor must be covered in water.

'Here I am,' Graham called. The light grew as he approached. 'Fortunately, there were a couple of torches in the car.'

He handed one to Penny.

The light from their torches reflected from the water covering the floor. It was only an inch or so deep but the sight of it filled Penny with dismay.

She turned her torch to the back of the storeroom. That was where the sound of the water was coming from but it was hard to make out anything from where they were standing.

After a moment's hesitation, she

stepped into the water, walking on tip-toe to try to keep her shoes as dry as possible. She made her way through the storeroom.

'Graham, look here.'

At the back, there was a door leading to the road at the rear of the shop. She could see water coming under the door and streaming down the two steps into the storeroom.

She turned the chunky key in the lock.

Then, grasping the handle, she pressed it down and pulled the door open.

'No, Penny, wait!' Graham shouted when he realised what she was doing.

It was too late. A flood of water surged through the gap. The force of it sent Penny staggering backwards.

Graham grabbed her, dropping his torch in the process and the water swept through the storeroom.

'What have I done?' Penny yelled in disbelief.

'Help me!' Graham shouted, throwing himself at the door.

Penny hurried to his side, water rushing past her ankles.

'Push!' he shouted and both of them forced their weight against the door.

Slowly, much too slowly, they closed the gap. Penny couldn't believe the strength of the water but, with a final effort, they forced the door shut. Graham turned the key in the lock.

Penny leaned back against the door for a moment, recovering her breath.

'I can't believe I was so stupid.' She groaned. 'What an idiotic thing to do.'

'These things happen,' Graham said sympathetically. 'Don't worry about it.'

'I just wanted to see where the water was coming from. I didn't think . . .'

She shone her torch around the storeroom. The water was much higher now. Graham splashed through it to fetch his torch. Amazingly, it still worked.

'It could be worse. The water hasn't got into the shop itself.'

He pointed towards the entrance of the storeroom. The water hadn't quite reached the top of the step.

'We've got to stop it rising any higher.

Round the back!' Penny cried.

She splashed her way out of the store-room with Graham following close behind her. She hurried through the shop, grabbing her coat on the way.

She pulled it on as she ran outside.

'This way,' she shouted to Graham and they raced through the area of waste ground. There was a single track road running down the back of All And Sundry and a cascade of water was pouring down it. 'I never thought of checking the back of the shop,' Penny wailed. 'It didn't occur to me that water might get in that way.'

Graham gazed at the back entrance.

'We have to block the gap at the bottom of the door.'

Penny could feel a sense of panic building up inside her. Her feet were icy cold, she was soaking wet and she felt tired and weary.

Worse than any of that was the sense that she had taken on the responsibility of looking after All And Sundry and she had let her mum and dad down.

As she stood there in the rain with water splashing past in the road, a cloud of despair settled over her. She turned, tears mingling with the rain on her face.

'Oh, Graham, what are we going to do?'

He looked at her for a moment and then held out his arms.

'Hey, come here.'

It was as if everything else quietly faded into the background – her drenched feet, the flooded storeroom, the weather. All that existed was Graham's arms round her.

Her head sank on to his shoulder, her body leaning against his. The strain that had seemed like a crushing weight gradually faded away.

When eventually they moved apart, the darkness inside her had gone and she felt a strange sense of peace.

Graham held her by the shoulders and looked at her, seeing if she was all right.

Penny gazed back at him.

She felt strangely envious of the drops of rain rolling down his face. For a moment, she was filled with a longing to stretch out and take his cheeks in her hands.

He stepped back with a half-amused look.

'You're smiling. Why?'

Penny felt a blush warming her cheeks.

'I'll tell you one day.'

He shook his head and looked around.

'I've had an idea. I'll be back in a couple of minutes.'

'Me, too,' Penny said.

She felt suddenly invigorated, eager to get to grips with the situation.

They both hurried off, Graham towards LoPrice, Penny back into All And Sundry.

Her uncertainty was gone.

She hurried into the shop and through to the storeroom. She shone the torch around the shelves.

'There they are,' she muttered.

She had remembered seeing the large decorating sheets earlier. She grabbed them in her arms and carried them to the back door.

She began packing the sheets along the gap at the bottom of the door. She had to kneel down in the water and her trousers, already wet, were soon drenched. But she didn't care.

She got to her feet and saw Graham approaching, pushing a loaded wheelbarrow.

'Sandbags!' Penny exclaimed. 'Perfect.'

'We made up lots to protect LoPrice from the flooding,' he said, putting down the wheelbarrow. 'Fortunately, there are some left over. If we pack them around the door, it should stop the water getting in ... or most of it, anyway.'

Together, they lifted the heavy bags out of the wheelbarrow and placed them hard against the door.

'I'll go back and get another load,' Graham said, grabbing hold of the wheelbarrow. 'A few more should do it. I won't be long.'

Penny leaned back against the wall and closed her eyes for a moment, waves of weariness washing over her.

Her mind felt scattered and confused.

So many things had happened in such a short time. But somewhere deep inside, she felt a rich warm glow, and it had to do with Graham. Dealing with the flooding seemed to have brought them together somehow.

And she liked that a lot.

'Here we are,' he called, approaching with the wheelbarrow. 'This should be more than enough.'

They packed another layer of sandbags around the door and then stood back to look at the result. The rushing water was now pushed well back from the door.

Graham nodded.

'Hopefully that will have stopped it.'

He lifted the handles of the wheelbarrow.

There were still a few sandbags left.

'We can take these round to the front of the shop in case they're needed there.'

Having dumped the sandbags by the front entrance, they went to look at the back door of the shop from the inside. To their relief, the water was no longer coming down the steps.

Graham insisted they wait a good five minutes to make sure no more water was getting in before he finally declared himself satisfied. He turned to her with a smile.

'I think we've sorted it.'

'Thank goodness for that.'

He lifted two plastic buckets which were floating in the water.

'Let's get to work. We need to get rid of as much of this water as we can before it does any more damage.'

More hard work was the last thing Penny felt ready for but Graham's energy drove her on. He fetched a plastic rubbish bin from the back of the shop and placed it in the middle of the storeroom.

Then they began scooping water into the bin, using the buckets. After a while, Graham dragged the bin through to the kitchen and emptied the water down the sink and they started all over again.

Penny wasn't sure how long they worked.

Her arms seemed like lead weights,

she had lost all sensation in her feet and she felt grubby all over. But eventually their buckets started scraping across concrete.

Graham stood up, stretching his back.

'I think we've done as much as we can. There's nothing but mud left on the floor.'

Penny looked at the door at the back of the storeroom.

'There's still no more water coming in. Graham, I don't know how to thank you.'

He grinned at her, his cheeks smudged and grimy. Penny couldn't believe that he was still able to smile after all this time.

'You could make that cup of tea you offered me hours ago.'

In silence, Penny made them cups of tea and Graham sorted out some cake. Neither of them had any energy for chit-chat.

He nibbled on a slice of lemon drizzle.

'This is good,' he murmured.

She smiled.

'I told you so.' She went over to the

window. 'Graham, come and look.'

He came and stood beside her.

'What is it?'

She nodded at the street.

'The rain has stopped. It looks as if the storm is over.' She gazed at him for a long moment. 'We did it, Graham. We saved All And Sundry.'

You're Fired!

The water was swirling everywhere, black and icy cold. It swept her off her feet and she grabbed desperately at an object rushing past — a cardboard cut-out of Darth Vader.

'Help!' she cried as her head sank beneath the surface.

A hand grabbed at her, pulling. Arms were round her, strong and urgent.

'Darling,' Graham murmured, his eyes blazing, his hair drenched. He pressed his lips against hers.

It was the moment Penny had been longing for but her head sank beneath the water again. Her chest heaved as she sucked in desperate lungfuls of air.

She gazed upwards, wide-eyed in confusion. It was the ceiling, the familiar ceiling; she was in bed at home. Her thrashing heart slowly calmed as she closed her eyes again. It was just a weird dream.

The memories flickered through her mind. They still seemed so real — the dark water, Graham holding her, kissing her. She shook her head and climbed out of bed.

'I need a coffee.'

She checked her phone while she waited for the kettle to boil.

There were a couple of messages from Angela. The Surfing Shack had been affected by the storm as well. She and Jordy were planning to help with the clearing up there and then they'd come round to All And Sundry later.

Penny sat by the window, gazing out at Weale Bay as she sipped her coffee. It was a perfect morning. Fingers of pink and red stretched out across the sky. It was hard to believe how different things had been just a few hours before.

She thought back to the previous evening. Her body still ached from the effort of lugging the sandbags around and clearing the water from the storeroom. She looked at her nails and grimaced.

Then she thought of Graham. She

hadn't really considered it at the time, they had been too busy dealing with the emergency. But without him, she didn't know how she would have coped.

It wasn't just what he had done to help deal with the flooding. Afterwards, he had stayed with her until they were absolutely sure that there was no further risk of water getting into the shop. She had told him to go home — like her, he was soaked and filthy. But he had refused.

'I'm going nowhere. For a start, we need something to eat. I don't know about you but I'm starving.'

He fetched them both a burger and fries from the takeaway up the road and they shared the food over a cup of tea.

Penny couldn't think of a less romantic occasion. They had been cold and weary, wet clothes clinging to them, so dirty.

Yet it was as if something had happened between them. Nothing had been said, no declarations were made. When Graham drove her home, there was certainly no goodnight kiss as he dropped her off. But there had been a change.

A bond seemed to have formed between them which hadn't been there before.

Penny made her way slowly along the promenade, enjoying the morning. For once, she was in no hurry.

There were so many urgent jobs waiting for her at All And Sundry. Getting to the shop a few minutes later than usual wasn't going to make that much difference.

Anyway, she needed time to think. All of a sudden, her life had become full of complications.

It had seemed such a simple matter when she first offered to look after All And Sundry. She would spend a few weeks taking care of the shop while her dad recuperated and then, at the end of the summer, she would go back to university and things would return to normal.

But it wasn't turning out like that at all.

189

For a start, there was the way that All And Sundry seemed to have taken over her life.

She was so full of ideas for the shop.

A picture had been growing in her mind of what it could be like in the future — a unique business, a community hub, selling specialised goods, offering all kinds of services, gathering an eager following of enthusiastic customers both locally and through social media.

She realised that it was probably completely idealistic and impractical. She had no real experience or proper training in running a business.

But it was going to be so hard to forget all about it when she handed the shop back to her mum and dad.

Then there was Graham. Penny hadn't planned to become romantically involved with anyone. She was young and carefree, she enjoyed life. If she met another free spirit like herself then she would have been happy to have a bit of fun with him over the summer.

But it was different with Graham.

Nothing romantic had happened between them at all, yet Graham had established a firm place in her heart almost without her realising it.

She liked him, she trusted him, she wanted to get to know him better. And somehow, even though nothing had been said between them, she knew that he felt the same.

Flo was already waiting at the doorway of the shop.

'You shouldn't be here this early, Flo,' Penny chided her. 'You're not due for another hour.'

'I've been so worried about the shop, Miss Penny. Si said the flooding in some of the roads was terrible. And I see you've got sandbags here.' She pointed at the two which Graham had left by the door.

Penny looked at them ruefully.

'Things were all right here at the front of the shop. It was at the back that we had the problems.' Penny unlocked the door and pushed it open. 'Be prepared for a bit of a mess.'

In fact, the shop and café area hadn't

been badly affected apart from some muddy footprints. But it was very different when they headed through to the back.

'The kitchen is a disaster area. We had to get rid of water from the storeroom and the only place it could go was down the kitchen sink. The water was filthy.'

'I don't think it's as bad as it seems,' Flo said, looking around. 'Not here in the kitchen, anyway. The dirt is mostly on the surface. But I'll have to give the whole room a good clean, top to bottom, before I think about doing any more baking.'

Penny nodded.

'It's the storeroom which is the real problem. That got properly flooded. The electricity will need fixing in there as well, but thankfully only that room was affected as it's on a separate electric circuit.'

The two of them gazed at the scene in silence. It was chaotic. The floor was damp and muddy, there was a musty smell in the air and the contents were scattered about all over the place.

'I don't know what we're going to do.

I'm not sure that anything much can be saved apart from what's on the shelves.

And we'll have to move that out quickly before it becomes affected by the damp.'

For a moment, Penny felt over-whelmed by the task facing them. All kinds of decisions needed to be made, decisions which were too important for her to make on her own.

Yet the last thing she wanted was to worry her parents about the business.

She sighed to herself, unsure where to start.

'How about if we sort out the front shop first?' Flo suggested. 'It's just the floor needing cleaned there. Then I can get to work on the kitchen while you look after the customers.'

Penny looked around uncertainly.

'I wondered if it might be simplest just to shut up the shop for the day so that we're free to concentrate on getting everything back to rights?'

'Goodness, no, Miss Penny, there's no need for that. We'll manage to sort things out between us. Now, let me get a mop and bucket for that floor.'

Penny smiled to herself. Normally, she was the decisive one, while Flo waited to be told what to do.

Flo buzzed about, full of energy, and it wasn't long before the floor was sparkling and the shop was ready to receive its first customers.

Penny found herself thinking of that first morning in charge when hardly anyone had come into the shop, at least to begin with.

Now there was a steady stream of people buying groceries, having their cuppas and cake, sitting on the deckchairs outside.

There were children getting their names on biscuits, people taking selfies of themselves with the cardboard cutouts — a cheerful little community shop, full of life and chatter.

She tidied up one of the outside tables and two children asked if she would take a picture of them with the R2D2 cut-out.

'Of course.' She smiled and waited in amusement as they put a sunhat on the robot's head and equipped him with a bucket and spade.

She was just waiting for the children to agree how to position themselves when she heard a sharp voice behind her.

'I want a word with you.'

Howard France was standing there, a cold look on his face.

'I'll just be a minute,' Penny smiled.

'I want a word with you now!'

Penny felt a surge of irritation.

'In a minute,' she retorted, turning her back on him firmly.

It was childish, she knew, but she took her time with the photos of the children. She insisted on taking a few of them and it was only when the children had agreed that the results were satisfactory that she handed back the camera and waved goodbye.

She turned back to Howard France

with her sweetest smile.

'Now, how can I help you?'

His cheeks were tinged with anger.

'A few minutes ago, I was speaking to one of our delivery drivers when I noticed some sandbags at the back of your shop.'

Penny nodded.

'They were lifesavers last night. Water was getting into the storeroom. Without the sandbags, the whole shop might have been flooded out.'

He pointed at the two by the entrance.

'And there are more here, I see.'

Penny nodded.

'Fortunately, these ones weren't needed.'

His voice was quiet but intense.

'If I'm not mistaken, those are our sandbags.'

'What?'

'LoPrice employees spent a great deal of time preparing sandbags in case they were needed during the storm. They were stacked at the back of the shop.'

Penny was looking at him in confusion.

'I'm not sure what you're getting at.'

He leaned closer, his eyes narrowing.

'I'm getting at the fact that, last night, LoPrice property was taken off the premises without permission.

Penny blinked.

'Are you accusing me of …?'

'I'm accusing you of theft. You took those sandbags knowing that they weren't yours.'

'That's a ridiculous thing to say.'

'It's true, though, isn't it? Those sandbags belonged to LoPrice, they were on LoPrice premises and you stole them for your own use.'

'No, she didn't.'

They both turned. Graham was standing there looking angry and unsettled.

'Penny didn't steal those sandbags. I brought them here from LoPrice.'

Howard France's mouth sagged open.

'You did?'

Graham nodded.

'It was an emergency. The sandbags weren't needed at LoPrice so I decided they could be put to better use at All

And Sundry.'

''You decided'?' Spittle flew from Howard France's mouth in his fury. 'You have no business making such a decision. You know what the LoPrice policy is towards All And Sundry. You knew perfectly well that I wouldn't have approved of such a decision.'

Graham shrugged.

'Nevertheless, I made it. I didn't feel that I had any option in the circumstances.'

Howard France was almost incandescent with rage.

'Well, I don't think that I have any option in these circumstances,' he snarled.

He raised a finger and pointed it straight at Graham.

'You're fired!'

I've Had Enough

Penny watched in disbelief as Howard France strode off up the road. She turned to Graham.

'He can't do that. You've got to stop him!'

But Graham just stood there shaking his head. Penny grabbed his arm.

'You have rights. You have to fight this.'

He looked at her with a resigned expression.

'To be honest, if he hadn't fired me, I was going to give up the job anyway. I've had enough of him.' He gazed up the road where Howard France was disappearing into LoPrice. 'I suppose I should go after him and collect my things.'

Penny sighed in frustration.

'Well, how about a cup of coffee first?' She looked around. 'We're getting a bit short on cake but there are still a couple of Flo's flapjacks left.'

He grinned.

'Now you're talking.'

One of the tables inside was free. Graham sat down at it while Penny sorted out the coffees. There were no customers waiting to be served so she joined him.

For a few moments, they just sat in silence. So much had happened over the past 24 hours. It was as if they both needed to get their bearings.

Penny gazed at him as he looked down at his coffee. She wondered about their relationship. She hadn't been sure about him at first. For a while, she had doubted that he was someone she could trust.

That was because I didn't know him, she thought. But I know him now.

He looked up and held her gaze. It was as if he was searching for something in her eyes. He stretched across the table and put his hand on hers. Penny's heart began to pound. She turned her hand so that their palms were together.

Neither of them said anything, they didn't need to. In that simple gesture, some sort of commitment had been made. Penny looked at him, at his dear face. Something inside her was singing with joy.

'What did Howard France mean,' she asked, 'when he spoke of LoPrice's policy towards All And Sundry?'

He shook his head.

'Do you remember the first time we met?'

Penny grinned.

'My first day looking after the shop, and you were there on the waste ground all set to buy us out.'

He grimaced.

'I really did think that Bill and Maisie had decided to sell up All And Sundry — that was what Howard France told me. I would never have dreamed of taking details of the property otherwise.'

Graham broke off a bit of his flapjack.

'He said that LoPrice needed to get in there quickly before the property had been put on the market so that it got a good deal. He even suggested that Bill's heart attack might make it possible to squeeze down the price. Your mum and dad might be willing to accept a speedy offer so that they had one less thing to worry about.'

Graham gave a sigh.

'I should have realised then what sort of person he was. I'm sorry, Penny.'

'There's no need to apologise. The man's a toad, that's all there is to it.'

He nodded.

'I won't argue with that.'

Graham explained that once Howard France realised that All And Sundry wasn't being sold, he did all that he could to put pressure on the shop.

He was the one who had contacted the Trading Standards officers about the footballs.

He had decided to undercut the prices in All And Sundry's café to try to tempt away its customers.

And he had instructed the delivery drivers to park outside the shop with their engines running.

'Though I didn't know about that until later,' Graham said. 'All along, his aim has been to try to put All And Sundry out of business. I didn't like the idea at all but I didn't think there was much I could do about it … until last night.

'I knew that he wouldn't want the spare sandbags to be used to help All And Sundry but I'd had enough. Being competitive is one thing. Refusing to help a neighbouring business in trouble through no fault of its own is something else altogether.'

He smiled.

'So here we are.'

A couple of customers came into the shop.

'I'll be back in a moment,' Penny said.

The customers only wanted a few groceries and she soon returned.

'I've loved all the ideas you've had for the shop,' Graham went on.

He laughed and it was as if his whole face lit up.

'They made Howard France so angry! He reckoned you were just some student who knew nothing about business. He thought he'd be able to trample all over you.

'But you had an answer to everything

he tried. It drove him mad.'

'Good,' Penny retorted with satisfaction.

She looked at him.

'But what are you going to do now?'

He shrugged.

'Get another job, I suppose. To be honest, I've been thinking about it for a while.

Working under Howard France hasn't been a very pleasant experience and I've been putting out a few feelers.

'A couple of other businesses have suggested that, if ever I'm looking for another job, I should apply to them. Fingers crossed, it shouldn't be too long before I find something else.'

He finished his coffee and popped the last bit of flapjack into his mouth.

'However, that's more than enough sitting around for one day. I'll go and fetch my stuff from LoPrice and make sure that I'm getting every penny that I'm due from them.'

He looked at her thoughtfully.

'Then, how about if I come back and

give you a hand here? I noticed Flo working away in the back. The storeroom must be in a right state — maybe I could help with tackling the mess.'

'I can't ask you to do that.' Penny frowned. 'You've done more than enough for us already.'

He shrugged.

'The alternative is going back to my flat and watching daytime TV. Anything has to be better than that.'

He got to his feet with a grin.

'With a bit of luck and if I work really hard, I might be offered another of Flo's flapjacks.'

Penny stepped forward and gave him a quick hug. It felt like the right thing to do.

'That's a deal.'

It was about half an hour later when Graham returned. Penny asked how his meeting with Howard France had gone but he was noncommittal.

She got the impression that it had been stormy.

He insisted on getting straight on with

tackling the mess in the storeroom. Since the job badly needed doing and both she and Flo were otherwise occupied, Penny didn't protest too much.

She was kept well-occupied over the course of the morning dealing with customers.

Then Angela turned up with Jordy around midday.

'I'm sorry that I haven't been around but Jordy and I have been helping get the Surfing Shack back on its feet.'

'It got flooded yesterday,' Jordy explained. 'Fortunately not too much damage was done but we had to get everything out of there and cleaned up before it could get back into business.'

'It's mostly done now,' Angela added, 'and there are plenty of other helpers there so we thought we'd come and see how things are going at All And Sundry.'

'Well, the Surfing Shack wasn't the only place that got flooded yesterday,' Penny said.

Angela looked at her in shock.

'You don't mean …?'

Penny nodded and Angela groaned.

'And I wasn't here to help! I am so sorry.'

'Don't worry. Things worked out OK.'

Angela gazed around as if looking for signs of damage.

Then her eyes widened in astonishment. She pointed towards the back of the shop.

'Hang on a minute. Did I just see …?'

Penny felt her cheeks flush.

Angela gazed at her intently.

'Exactly what is going on here?'

Penny sighed. She knew that Angela wouldn't give up until she had uncovered every single detail.

'You'd better sit down. This may take a while.'

Jordy pulled his guitar from round his shoulder.

'In that case, I'll go and do a bit of busking outside, if that's all right.'

'Of course.' Penny smiled.

She and Angela found themselves seats and she began to explain.

'I suppose it started yesterday when the water began rising higher and higher on the street outside.'

It was two cups of coffee and a number of interruptions to deal with customers later when Penny finally got to the end of the story. Angela sat back in her seat, shaking her head in amazement.

'So Howard France is a creep and Gorgeous Graham is a hero.' Then she frowned. 'But I don't understand what he's doing out the back of this shop. Surely he's not working here?'

'He is, in a way. Well, not exactly. That is, he's working but … I'm not sure how to put it.'

'You're making about as much sense as a box of doughnuts,' Angela muttered, getting to her feet. 'There's only one solution.'

She headed for the back of the shop.

'No, hang on,' Penny called after her. 'Angela, wait a minute!'

Angela had made her way straight to the storeroom. Following her, Penny was amazed by the difference Graham had already made. The back door was open to let in the air and the items on the shelves were gone.

The rest of the items were packed together in one corner allowing Graham to clean the rest of the floor properly.

Angela strode over to him.

'Hi, there, I'm Angela.'

He wiped his hand on a rag and the two of them shook hands.

'Nice to meet you, Angela. I'm Graham.'

'I'm a friend of Penny's.'

There was a moment of hesitation.

'Me, too,' Graham said.

He glanced at Penny over Angela's shoulder and their gaze held for a moment.

Angela began to fan herself with her hand.

'Is it my imagination or has it suddenly got very warm in here?'

Penny turned away in some confusion.

Angela began pushing her back towards the shop.

'Off you go.'

'What?'

Angela took her coat off.

'I'm going to stay and help Graham with whatever he's doing.'

She smiled at him innocently.

'We have such a lot to talk about.'

'Hang on ...' Penny began.

But Angela was having none of it and Penny, in resignation, went back to the shop. When Angela was on a roll, there was no point trying to resist her.

★ ★ ★

'That man is such a hottie.' Angela sighed.

She lounged back in the deckchair as people wandered about the outside area chatting and laughing. Si had something sizzling on the barbecue and Jordy was playing his guitar and singing gently in the background.

'Do you mean Jordy?'

'Well, obviously Jordy's a hottie but he's not who I was thinking of.'

'You must mean Eric, then?' Penny

suggested innocently.

The informal party on the waste ground had started after the shop had shut up for the day and Brian and Eric had appeared out of nowhere to join them.

Angela took a sip of wine.

'Now, I like Eric. I wouldn't be surprised if he was a secret hottie in his day — one of those quiet guys who sneaks into your heart without you realising it.'

She glanced round at Penny.

'A bit like your Graham.'

Penny was about to protest that he wasn't 'her' Graham, but that wasn't true.

Although nothing had been said between them, she felt completely bound to him.

'I like him,' Angela murmured.

They both looked at Graham. He was listening politely while Brian explained something to him in great detail.

He looked their way and his eyes met Penny's in an amused, resigned expression.

Angela turned to her.

'And he likes you — a lot.'

Penny's stomach seemed to flip over.

'Why, did he say something?'

'Nothing in particular. But every time you were mentioned, he seemed to glow.'

A bit like I'm doing now, Penny thought.

'And he doesn't mind a bit of hard work. He kept us both at it all afternoon.'

'I'm so grateful to you,' Penny said.

She saw Graham make his way over.

'You managed to escape from Brian, then?'

'He was explaining you must always sieve your flour when you're baking.'

She grinned.

'Fascinating.'

'But I forgot to give you this.'

He handed her a sheet of paper which was covered with neat scribbles.

'Angela and I removed and cleaned up everything that we thought could still be sold in the shop. And I made this list of all the other items. You'll need it for the insurance.

'The policy should allow you to claim back on any damage. With luck, it'll also pay for dehumidifiers to deal with the damp in the storeroom as well.'

Penny gazed at the list in silence. She didn't know what sort of insurance the shop had. She just hoped that it wasn't something her father had cut back on.

'Not everything is on the list,' Graham went on. 'Some items weren't damaged by the flood but they're rubbish. A decision must be made on what to do with them.'

'If it was up to me, I would just chuck the lot,' Penny murmured. 'Have a complete clear-out and start again.'

But she knew that it wasn't her decision to make. She grimaced.

'I have to speak to Mum and Dad about this — in fact, about All And Sundry in general. And it's not the sort of conversation you can have over the phone.'

She looked at Graham. 'I need to go and see them.'

It's Time to Sell Up

Penny's throat felt ragged and raw. Each breath was agony and she wasn't sure how many more steps were left in her legs.

'Not long to go,' Bill called back. 'It's just round this next corner.'

'Slow down, Bill,' Maisie urged. 'It's not a race.'

It was a glorious Sunday morning and the three of them were toiling up Bezley Crag, the hill behind Auntie May's house.

When Bill had suggested that they take the path to the top, he had made it sound like a casual stroll. But as they approached the summit waves of pain were gripping Penny's legs.

'I'm not up to this,' she muttered.

'Here we are,' Bill said, coming to a stop.

He looked round. 'Isn't this wonderful?'

Penny dropped her backpack to the ground and collapsed on to a handy rock. It was a relief not to be walking any longer.

'It's like a feast for your eyes. I reckon this must be just about the best view in the world.'

Penny wasn't the slightest bit interested in views right at that moment. Her chest was burning, her throat was sore, her thighs were shaking. She felt as if she had just run an uphill marathon carrying a bag of stones on her back.

'You really are feeling better, aren't you, Dad?' She gazed at him.

Penny had taken the train to the Lake District the day before. It was obvious that she needed to have a proper conversation with Bill and Maisie about the future of All And Sundry.

She also wanted to see her dad. His phone calls recently had been so bright and cheery. He sounded great and he claimed that he was recovering well. But she wanted to see him with her own eyes.

Her original plan had been to close

All And Sundry so that she could make the journey. It would only be for one day as the shop didn't open on Sundays.

However, Flo, Angela and Graham wouldn't hear of it.

'It's Saturday, it's going to be a gorgeous day according to the forecast and the town is heaving,' Angela protested. 'All And Sundry needs to stay open.'

'I've got the kitchen up and running again, Miss Penny,' Flo added. 'We've got lots of cakes to sell.'

Graham nodded.

'I'm sure that the three of us can manage for one day.'

'I can't expect you to look after All And Sundry.'

'I want to,' Graham said firmly. 'We all do. If you close All And Sundry, even for a day, it'll be a victory for Howard France. We can't allow that.'

In the end, Penny had no choice but to give in. She would take the train to the Lake District first thing on Saturday morning and then return on Sunday evening.

In fact, she was glad that they had insisted on keeping All And Sundry open. She suspected that Howard France was more determined than ever to take over the property. Closing the shop even for one day would only encourage him.

That was a real concern for Penny. There were all kinds of ways in which he could use LoPrice's economic muscle to put pressure on All And Sundry.

She worried that, if he was resolute enough, Bill and Maisie wouldn't be able to stand up against him.

'What do you think?' Bill smiled at Penny, indicating the view.

She looked at the farms, streams and villages spread out below them like a patchwork quilt.

'It's glorious, Dad.'

'When we visited your Auntie May in the past, I don't think I really appreciated just how beautiful the Lake District is.'

Maisie snorted.

'That was because you were always so desperate to get back to All And Sundry.

You could never be away from that shop for more than a day without getting ants in your pants.'

Bill nodded.

'You're right. The shop was all I could think about. It was an obsession, really.' He shook his head. 'Foolish of me.'

Penny gazed at her dad in disbelief.

'Well, you've changed your attitude since you had your heart attack!'

He shrugged.

'Going through an experience like that makes you rethink your priorities. Maisie and I worked so hard on the shop to keep it going. Long hours, constant stress, hardly any proper breaks. And why? What was it for?'

'It hasn't been all bad.' Maisie smiled. 'We've made some good friends over the years.'

Bill nodded.

'Absolutely, it's been great in lots of ways. But we need to be thinking about the rest of our lives now and how we can make the most of them.'

He looked around, taking in the view.

'I've enjoyed staying here so much. And I feel years younger. I'm getting regular exercise, I'm eating more sensibly, I'm sleeping well …'

'And you've started fishing again.'

Bill laughed.

'I'm not sure it counts as fishing when you never catch anything.'

Penny gazed at him, shaking her head.

'I can't believe I'm hearing this, Dad. You seem so chilled.'

He nodded slowly.

'I feel chilled. And do you know what the best thing is? Maisie and I are spending time together. Not working in the shop all hours but relaxing and enjoying each other's company.'

He stretched out a hand and Maisie took it in hers with a smile.

Penny felt tears welling up in her eyes. Of course, she had always known that her mum and dad loved each other. They had met at school, married early and been together all their adult lives. There had never been anyone else for either of them.

But they hadn't been in the habit of making open demonstrations of affection. To see them now, sharing their love for each other, moved her more than she could have imagined.

'Come here, you two,' she said, stretching out her arms for a hug. 'You've got me crying.'

'Tell me more about Graham,' Maisie said as they started making their way back down the hill. 'He seems to have been very helpful when the shop was flooded.'

'Surely you know him?' Penny frowned.

'Just to say hello to. To be honest, Howard France was never very friendly towards us. He didn't encourage any of the LoPrice staff to have much to do with us.'

'Graham is nice,' Penny said. 'I like him.'

Even as she spoke the words, she realised how inadequate they were. Graham had become so much more to her than just a casual friend.

* * *

Auntie May had a light lunch waiting for them when they got back down the hill.

Penny was amused by how Bill accepted this without complaint. In the past, Sunday lunch for him would have meant a proper roast with all the trimmings but now he seemed happy with a bowl of lentil soup followed by quiche with a bit of salad.

He really had changed.

They sat on the patio with their coffees and enjoyed the view.

'This is all very idyllic.' Penny sighed. 'But I have to get the train back to Weale in a couple of hours and there are things we need to sort out before I go.'

Bill glanced at Maisie.

'There was something we wanted to discuss, too. But you go first.'

Penny had already told them all about the flood.

'We recovered some of the items from the storeroom. But most of the contents were damaged by the water. I wondered what the insurance situation was?'

Bill grimaced.

'Insurance was one of the areas we had to cut back on but any damage to the property from the flooding will still be covered.'

'So the insurance company should deal with the dampness in the storeroom — and the electricity?'

Bill nodded.

'I imagine they'll organise some industrial dehumidifiers to dry it up. The trouble is that the contents of the storeroom aren't covered by our policy.'

Maisie snorted.

'Most of the stuff in there is rubbish, anyway.'

Penny expected a protest from Bill. He had always insisted that the items in the storeroom would all come in useful some day. Instead, he just laughed.

'You're probably right. To be honest, you might as well get rid of anything that was damaged by the flooding.'

Penny gaped at him.

'What, just chuck it?'

Bill shrugged.

'That seems the simplest solution.'

Penny was stunned. It was the last thing she would have expected him to say, though it was exactly what she had suggested to Graham should happen.

'If it was up to me, I would hire a skip and dump the lot,' she had said. 'I would clear out the storeroom completely.'

He had agreed.

'It could actually be a really useful space. The café area could be expanded to fill the main shop while the storeroom could become where you put goods for sale. All And Sundry's floor space would be doubled in one go.'

It hadn't occurred to Penny that her dad would even consider the idea. Yet here he was, agreeing to have a clearout of the storeroom without an argument.

She turned to him eagerly. With Bill in this mood, perhaps it was her opportunity to tell him about some of the other ideas she'd had for the shop.

'We also thought about expanding the kitchen area. It would be great if we could build up the café's menu to include sandwiches and light lunches — they're really popular with holidaymakers.

'We've made some links with a local bakery and their specialist breads are selling well. If we produced sandwiches made from them then I think we could be on to a winner, particularly now that we're building up our social media profile. People will come to Weale-On-Sea already knowing about All And Sundry. They'll look out for us.'

Bill and Maisie glanced at each other.

'It sounds as if you've been giving this a lot of thought.'

'That's not all,' Penny went on eagerly. 'I reckon the area of waste ground at the side of the shop could turn out to be a gold mine. There's plenty of space there and the view over the bay is spectacular. If we could use it to attract families, it could be a real boost to the business.'

She explained her idea of fitting an awning to the side of the shop to provide shade from the sun, then told them about Graham's suggestion for a 24-hour vending machine. She had begun exploring the possibility of a small crazy golf course; having regular spots for buskers to entertain the clientele; party nights with karaoke and a barbecue.

'Woah, woah,' Bill said, breaking in on her torrent of enthusiasm. 'Slow down a bit, Penny.'

Penny laughed.

'I just think that All And Sundry has so much potential. There are so many ways the business could be developed.'

Bill and Maisie glanced at each other. They turned to Penny, neither of them looking very comfortable.

Penny frowned.

'What is it?'

'We've been having some ideas, too, dear,' Maisie said quietly.

Bill nodded.

'We've been thinking a lot about the future over the last few weeks.'

'That's good.'

'This is such a lovely part of the world. It's so peaceful and quiet. The thought of retiring here suddenly seems attractive.'

'Retiring?'

Bill nodded.

'It's the right time for us. And of course you'll soon be off somewhere making your own life when you finish at university.'

'What are you saying?'

Bill stretched over and took Maisie's hand.

'We've talked about it a lot and we've come to a decision. We're going to sell up.'

Penny gazed at them in disbelief.

'Sell All And Sundry?'

Bill nodded.

'It's a good site for development. We should get a decent price.'

'It's time to think of ourselves for a change,' Maisie went on. 'We've had enough of working all hours. So we're going to sell up and retire.'

★ ★ ★

Penny gazed blindly out of the train carriage window. A few weeks ago, the idea

226

of Bill and Maisie retiring would have delighted her.

But over the last few weeks everything had changed. She had enjoyed looking after the shop. She found that she was good at it and at coming up with new ideas for the future and the many ways All And Sundry could be developed. Now all that was over.

She stepped wearily out of the carriage at Weale-On-Sea and made her way slowly along the platform, miserable and lost.

'Hi, Penny.'

She stopped.

'Graham,' she whispered in disbelief.

He hesitated, then opened his arms. She dropped her bag and walked straight into them. She was lost no longer.

One Other Possibility

They sat next to each other on the sea wall, the reflection of the moon rippling across the water. Penny was holding tightly on to Graham's hand. That made eating from the carton of fish and chips on her lap more difficult but she had no intention of letting go of his hand.

In fact, she thought it was possible that she might never let go of his hand for the rest of her life.

She leaned gently against his shoulder.

'How did you know which train I was on?'

'I didn't. So I met them all.'

She looked at him.

'You did that for me?'

He nodded. After a moment, she raised her head and their lips met. It was possible that she might not stop kissing this lovely man for the rest of her life, either, she decided after a while.

He pulled away with a smile.

'You'd better finish your fish and chips before they get cold.'

She popped a chip into her mouth. It had been his idea. She'd been too miserable to have anything to eat on the journey and had suddenly realised that she was hungry.

So he bought her a takeaway and they sat together on the seafront while she ate it and told him about the trip.

'It sounds as if the Lake District has done wonders for your dad.'

'I couldn't believe how well he was. He was racing up and down the hills like a twenty-year-old.'

'That must be a relief for Maisie. I know how worried she was.'

'It was his attitude which amazed me the most. All these years, everything in his life has taken second place to All And Sundry. But that has completely changed. All he cares about now is that he and Maisie make the most of their retirement.'

'They deserve the chance to enjoy

life for a change.'

Penny smiled.

'It's funny seeing them now that they're not stressed out by running All And Sundry. They're so happy together, so in love.'

Graham gave her hand a squeeze.

'If you're finished with that, will I chuck the wrapper in the bin?'

He tied the container up in its plastic bag so that the seagulls couldn't get at it and dropped it into a nearby bin.

Penny watched him, a slight smile on her face. She wasn't really sure what she thought or felt; it was too soon and too much had been happening. But there was a glowing sense of joy deep within her.

It was as if she had found something she had been looking for all her life without even realising it.

He held out a hand.

'Shall we go for a wander along the beach?'

She kicked off her shoes. The sand

felt so good between her toes, still warm after the heat of the day.

His arm settled over her shoulder and she cuddled up to him as they walked. It felt as if they had been carefully designed to fit perfectly together.

Penny talked quietly about All And Sundry and the place it had always had in her life.

'The shop seems a bit tatty and out of date now, but it wasn't always like that. It was a thriving business when I was young. Mum and Dad had two other assistants apart from Flo in the summer months and it was always full of customers.'

She looked out at the sea. The water was like grey silk. It seemed so peaceful. The waves barely made a sound as they rolled up the beach and came to a stop.

She sighed.

'The trouble was that Dad never really changed with the times. Life is so much

harder for small shops these days. All

And Sundry has been failing for a long time.'

'And they have finally decided to sell up?' Graham asked.

Penny nodded.

'It was actually my Auntie May's suggestion. Her house is far too big for her on her own. My Uncle Sandy died a few years ago and their three children have all left home. She loves the Lake District, though, and she's been thinking for a while about moving to somewhere smaller.

'I sense a 'but' coming.

Penny smiled.

'The three of them get on so well together and they've really enjoyed these last few weeks. So Auntie May suggested that she keep the house and that Mum and Dad move in with her permanently.'

'Sounds like a great idea,' Graham replied. He looked at her. 'How do you feel about it?

Penny gave a rueful laugh.

'I've been encouraging them to do

something like this for years. It was such a struggle for them trying to keep All And Sundry going. If they'd made the decision a couple of months ago, I would have danced in delight.'

Graham grinned.

'I'd like to see you doing that.'

Penny kissed him instead.

'But you've changed your mind?' he suggested as they carried on along the beach, hand in hand.

'Not about Mum and Dad retiring, I'm really happy about that. It's just that . . .'

Penny found herself thinking about everything that had happened with All And Sundry. She'd found looking after it so exciting. Every day she seemed to wake up filled with new ideas and buzzing with an eagerness to try them out.

She sighed.

'I'm going to miss running the shop.'

'Couldn't you still do that? Wouldn't your parents be happy to let you carry on?'

'It's my degree. I've worked so hard

on it over the past couple of years. I wouldn't want to give it up now.'

'I can understand that,' Graham murmured.

'Anyway, if they're going to move, they'll have to sell the shop. They need the money. It's not as if they've managed to accumulate much in the way of savings over the years.'

They wandered slowly along the beach.

For a while, they became distracted by the gentle twining and intertwining of their fingers. Then Penny found herself compelled to kiss Graham for a bit.

She rolled up her trouser legs and began walking through the shallows.

'I've enjoyed looking after All And Sundry so much. I only took it on reluctantly but I've loved the experience.'

Disappointment settled over her.

'I didn't expect that.'

They walked on in silence for a bit and then Graham stopped. He looked at her as if he was searching her eyes, trying to come to a decision.

'What is it?'

He took both her hands in his.

'Of course, there is one other possibility.'

* * *

'It's a mad idea, Graham!' Penny protested. 'You're a supermarket manager. You can't take over a little shop like All And Sundry.'

'It wouldn't just be me taking over the shop, Penny, it would be the two of us.'

'But I still have a year to go at university.'

'Of course you should complete your degree, but I could run All And Sundry in the meantime. And you would still be involved in the holidays and maybe the occasional weekend if you came back.'

Penny smiled to herself. If Graham was staying in Weale-On-Sea then she suspected that she would be returning on more than the occasional weekend.

But then she frowned.

'How would it work out financially?'

He shrugged.

'I have some savings; a loan could be arranged. . .'

Penny looked at him uncertainly. He took her hands and held them firmly.

'Penny, there are all kinds of practical issues that would have to be dealt with. But none of them would be impossible to overcome.

'I just feel that the two of us would be a perfect partnership for running a shop like All And Sundry. I've got business experience and training while you have such fantastic ideas. And we get on so well together.'

'We do, don't we?' Penny murmured.

'If we believe in each other, there's no end to the possibilities. I'm suggesting that you and I join together and take All And Sundry into a whole new future. So what do you say?'

She gazed at him. His face was alive with excitement, an excitement that she felt too.

She threw her arms round his neck.

'I say 'Yes'.'

To the Future

'I can't believe how different it all is. This is fantastic, Penny.'

The party was starting to go with a swing. Maisie had mentioned in passing to Angela that she quite liked 'The Birdie Song'. To her horror, Angela had immediately dragged her up on to the little stage.

The two of them were now leading the actions of the song with Jordy playing and a crowd of people up on their feet and dancing.

Bill gazed around in amazement.

'You and Graham have done wonders with this patch of ground. It was just a rubbish dump before.'

Penny smiled.

'I am pleased with the way it has turned out.'

There were a dozen tables scattered around the outside area, all with their cheerful tablecloths and little posies of wild flowers. A new gazebo had been erected along with a colourful awning stretching out from the wall. There were palm trees in pots and deckchairs to give a real feeling of summer at the beach.

In one corner, children were bouncing enthusiastically on the trampoline and playing in the sand pit.

'With the view of the bay, it's the perfect place for a relaxing cuppa or an ice-cream. And now that we've built up the menu, it's proving really popular.' Penny smiled.

Bill enveloped her in a hug.

'You've made me so proud, Penny.'

'The Birdie Song' had come to an end and Maisie, now well into her stride, was persuading Jordy to move on to 'The Macarena'.

'Come on, Bill!' Angela shouted. 'Come and dance with your wife.'

Bill turned away in horror.

'There's Brian and Eric. I must say hello to them. Speak to you later, Pen.'

Penny glanced around. Everywhere she looked, there was the sound of chatter and laughter. She and Graham had tried to spread the word as widely as possible; everyone was invited to the relaunch of All And Sundry.

Their efforts had clearly been successful.

Inside and out, the place was heaving with customers, locals, friends, even passers-by. And they all seemed to be having a great time.

She smiled to herself as she spotted Graham talking earnestly with a bearded man whom she didn't recognise. They would be discussing business, she was sure of it.

'This is the perfect opportunity to network and build up our contacts, Penny,' he had said when they were planning the party. 'Get people here in a relaxed atmosphere where everyone is enjoying themselves and they'll want to become involved in what we're doing at All And Sundry.'

He had been right, as he was about so many things. A smile played around her mouth. The two of them made such a good partnership, in all kinds of ways.

She looked around, wondering if she should be networking with someone.

She noticed a striking middle-aged woman gazing thoughtfully at the shop front. A large screen had now been fixed permanently to the wall by the window.

Normally, it had a constantly changing menu, showing which items were selling the best that day, reviews of Flo's latest efforts by members of the Cake Club, customers' musical requests, selfies which people had uploaded and so on.

But today it was simply displaying a stream of online messages wishing All And Sundry the best of luck in the future. Penny would be replying to every one of the messages later. It may have involved a lot of work but #AllAndSundry was proving a real success in spreading the word about the business.

'Hi, there.' Penny smiled.

The woman looked at her thoughtfully.

'Hello.' She nodded at the screen. 'I noticed this the other day when I was passing the shop. It looked like a really interesting idea.'

'We're still working on it,' Penny said enthusiastically. 'But the screen is like a virtual window on the business. It gives passers-by an insight into everything that's going on at All And Sundry. We show all kinds of things on it — pictures people have taken of themselves at the shop, music that Jordy over there has played, any latest special offers.'

'Sounds great. I may just pinch that idea.'

She smiled at Penny. 'I haven't introduced myself. I'm Florinda Strang. I'm the new manager at LoPrice next door.'

'Penny Sullivan.' The two women shook hands. 'I heard that Howard France had left.'

Florinda raised an eyebrow.

'He's been 'promoted' to a post in our northern office.'

She glanced at the party for a few moments.

'I like the atmosphere you've created here. There's a real sense of community. That's very valuable in a business.'

Penny felt pleased at the compliment.

'That's good of you to say so. We're trying to develop All And Sundry in all kinds of ways. I don't suppose they'll all be successful.'

'You'll never achieve anything in business if you're not prepared to risk failing from time to time.'

'I completely agree,' Penny said eagerly.

'You learn so much more from your mistakes.'

Florinda looked at Penny sharply for a few moments.

'I get the impression that there have been problems between LoPrice and All And Sundry in the past.'

Penny smiled ruefully.

'You might say that.'

'Well, I want to change that. We're not threats to each other. We're completely different businesses. Instead of trying to compete, we should be working together.'

'How do you mean?'

Florinda gestured up and down the road.

'We have a community here in Beach Road, or we could have. A dozen different businesses all with the same aim in mind, to attract more customers.

'We could do that much more effectively if we worked together.'

Penny frowned.

'I'm not quite following you.'

Florinda shrugged.

'There are all kinds of possibilities. For instance, it won't be long before we're thinking about our Christmas sales. We could arrange to have the road closed one Saturday and have our own little Beach Road Winter Festival. Bands, bouncy castles, stalls. It wouldn't necessarily cost a lot but it would attract a lot of people and all our businesses would benefit.'

Penny gazed at her wide-eyed.

'That's a fantastic idea!'

'That's just the start of it. There are all kinds of things we could do if we were prepared to cooperate.'

Florinda smiled.

'Maybe we should get together and discuss it sometime?'

'Give me a time and place and I'll be there.'

'I'm glad we've sorted that out. Now, I wonder if you could direct me to the young man who left LoPrice recently to work at All And Sundry?'

'You mean Graham? Come and I'll introduce you.'

Graham had just said goodbye to his bearded companion.

'It's been great speaking to you, Callum. We'll be in touch soon.'

He turned to Penny eagerly.

'That was Callum Friend. He has a small shop in Torbeach along the coast which he's trying to develop. He really likes what we're doing here and he wants to set up an All And Sundry there.'

Penny's eyes widened in disbelief.

'That's amazing!'

Florinda stepped forward.

'You two clearly have a great deal to discuss. I just wanted to make myself known.'

Penny did the introductions and Florinda looked at Graham thoughtfully.

'I'd be sorry to think that there were any bad feelings between our two businesses. As I've been explaining to Penny, I think we should be working together.'

'There are no hard feelings on my side,' Graham said.

'I've been talking to people,' Florinda murmured. 'I get the impression that we lost a valuable member of staff when you left LoPrice.'

Penny put an arm round Graham's waist.

'Well, you can't have him back.' She smiled.

'I can see that.'

Florinda glanced at her watch.

'I need to get back to LoPrice. But I'm pleased that I've had this chance to meet the two of you. Hopefully, our two businesses have a productive future together.'

Penny and Graham stood arm-in-arm for a moment just gazing around. There were smiles everywhere, noisy chatter, peals of laughter.

'I have such a good feeling about this,' Penny murmured.

Graham nodded.

'Today has been a really good start for the new All And Sundry.'

'Hey, this isn't good enough — you're not drinking anything,' Angela cried, appearing out of the café with a tray of brimming champagne glasses. 'You're the ones throwing the party, you need to be setting an example. Take a glass so that I can go and serve Jordy. He's sounding thirsty.'

She hurried off and Penny glanced at Graham. There were times lately when she felt she was in the middle of a wonderful dream. Everything was turning out so well.

Just to convince herself, she moved against him.

He was real all right. Their lips met gently a moment later.

She was vaguely aware of someone whooping in the background, Jordy starting to play 'Happy Together', and people singing. But Penny wasn't really paying attention to anything else.

She and Graham lifted their glasses and clinked them together.

'To the future.'

We do hope that you have enjoyed reading this large print book.

Did you know that all of our titles are available for purchase?

We publish a wide range of high quality large print books including:
Romances, Mysteries, Classics
General Fiction
Non Fiction and Westerns

Special interest titles available in large print are:
The Little Oxford Dictionary
Music Book, Song Book
Hymn Book, Service Book

Also available from us courtesy of Oxford University Press:
Young Readers' Dictionary
(large print edition)
Young Readers' Thesaurus
(large print edition)

For further information or a free brochure, please contact us at:
Ulverscroft Large Print Books Ltd.,
The Green, Bradgate Road, Anstey,
Leicester, LE7 7FU, England.
Tel: (00 44) **0116 236 4325**
Fax: (00 44) **0116 234 0205**

TURPIN'S APPRENTICE

Sarah Swatridge

England, 1761. Charity Bell is the daughter of an inn keeper. Her two elder sisters are only interested in marrying well, whereas feisty Charity is determined to discover who the culprit is behind the most recent highwayman ambush. And by catching the highwayman, she aims to persuade Sir John to bring his family, and his wealth, to her village. It may also make the handsome Moses notice her!